PIPPA'S
iSLAND

BOOKS BY BELINDA MURRELL

Pippa's Island
Book 1: The Beach Shack Cafe
Book 2: Cub Reporters

The Locket of Dreams
The Ruby Talisman
The Ivory Rose
The Forgotten Pearl
The River Charm
The Sequin Star
The Lost Sapphire

The Sun Sword Trilogy
Book 1: The Quest for the Sun Gem
Book 2: The Voyage of the Owl
Book 3: The Snowy Tower

Lulu Bell
Lulu Bell and the Birthday Unicorn
Lulu Bell and the Fairy Penguin
Lulu Bell and the Cubby Fort
Lulu Bell and the Moon Dragon
Lulu Bell and the Circus Pup
Lulu Bell and the Sea Turtle
Lulu Bell and the Tiger Cub
Lulu Bell and the Pyjama Party
Lulu Bell and the Christmas Elf
Lulu Bell and the Koala Joey
Lulu Bell and the Arabian Nights
Lulu Bell and the Magical Garden
Lulu Bell and the Pirate Fun

BOOK 2

PIPPA'S iSLAND

CUB REPORTERS

BELINDA MURRELL

RANDOM HOUSE AUSTRALIA

A Random House book
Published by Penguin Random House Australia Pty Ltd
Level 3, 100 Pacific Highway, North Sydney NSW 2060
www.penguin.com.au

 Penguin
Random House
Australia

First published by Random House Australia in 2017

Addresses for the Penguin Random House group of companies can be found at
global.penguinrandomhouse.com/offices.

National Library of Australia
Cataloguing-in-Publication entry

Creator: Murrell, Belinda, author
Title: Cub reporters / Belinda Murrell
ISBN: 978 0 14378 368 8 (pbk)
Series: Murrell, Belinda. Pippa's Island; 2
Target audience: For primary school age
Subjects: Friendship – Juvenile fiction
          Coffee shops – Juvenile fiction

Cover and internal design by Christabella Designs
Cover and internal images: beautiful white beach Charcompix/Shutterstock;
happy golden retriever puppy otsphoto/Shutterstock; feet girl Alohaflaminggo/
Shutterstock; tourist traveler photographer Maria Savenko/Shutterstock; portrait
of a young girl Andrey Arkusha/Shutterstock; summer cards Ksenia Lokko/
Shutterstock; hand-drawn summer creative alphabet Ksenia Lokko/Shutterstock
Typeset by Midland Typesetters, Australia
Printed in Australia by Griffin Press, an accredited ISO AS/NZS 14001:2004
Environmental Management System printer

Penguin Random House Australia uses papers that are natural, renewable
and recyclable products and made from wood grown in sustainable forests.
The logging and manufacturing processes are expected to conform to the
environmental regulations of the country of origin.

For Emily, Ella and Meg.
My beautiful girls.
Thanks for your endless inspiration!

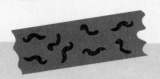

Have you ever really dreaded something? And then, when it happens, it's nowhere near as bad as you thought it would be? In fact, it turns out to be really incredible instead?

That happened to me. I'm a Kira Island girl now, but when Mum first told us we were moving here, I couldn't think of anything worse!

Kira Island is a tiny place on the other side of the world from where I grew up. No one's ever heard of it. It's postcard perfect - there are frangipanis and palm trees, turquoise water laps against coral-white beaches, and dolphins splash in the waves. The four of us moved here from London a few months ago to start a new life. My family is my mum, my brother, Harry, my sister, Bella, and me - Philippa Hamilton, but everyone calls me Pippa. The latest addition to our family is Summer, our new and very mischievous puppy.

Mum decided to spend our very last pennies to buy an old tumbledown boatshed on the beach at Kira Cove. Now it is called the Beach Shack, and is the newest, most beautiful cafe on the island. Our whole family worked for weeks to get it ready.

For the moment, we live in a tiny caravan in the back garden of my grandparents' cottage. The move was hard because we had to fly halfway around the world, change schools and leave all our friends behind us. At first I hated it. I thought I'd never fit in.

But now I have the best group of friends a girl could wish for. Together, we are the Sassy Sisters. There is Charlie Harper, a boho beach babe who loves to sing and play the guitar. Cici Lin, the cupcake queen, bakes the most delicious treats and is also the most stylish fashionista. Meg is the quietest but most caring. Cici calls Meg the Wildlife Warrior because she's on a personal mission to save the world. And then there's me - a regular girl just trying to fit in. Our club motto is 'Be bold! Be brave! And be full of happy spirit!'. And that's just what we are.

Pippa

PUPPY LOVE

Summer, our new puppy, looked up at me with adoring brown eyes. Between her paws was one of Mum's best shoes, which was covered in tiny tooth marks. The insole was in shreds all over the floor.

'Oh, Summer,' I said. 'You are so gorgeous and so wicked!'

Summer wagged her plumed tail madly and licked my fingers. When I tried to extract Mum's shoe, the puppy grabbed it with her needle-sharp teeth and shook her head from side to side, ripping the shoe more.

'Summer, it's not a game,' I said, hanging onto the shoe tightly. 'Mum will be furious!'

Then I remembered the command that Mum had taught us to say whenever Summer stole something she shouldn't have.

I let go of the shoe and used my sternest voice. 'Summer, leave it!'

Summer grabbed the shoe and ran for it instead. She hid under the caravan table and happily chewed away. I crawled in after her. Eventually I managed to wrestle the shoe off the puppy. But I doubted Mum would want to wear those shoes ever again.

Our golden retriever puppy was only ten weeks old. I'd named her Summer after our new home, because she is the colour of Kira Beach sand and endless sunshine. Mum gave her to Harry, Bella and me to say thank you for helping her renovate the old boatshed.

I think Summer was also a kind of bribe for the three of us, to help make up for everything that had happened. You see, none of us had wanted to leave London and move to Kira Island. First of all, my dad's investment business went bankrupt so we lost most of our money and had to sell our house. Dad became different after that – I think he thought he had let us all down. Then, when he was offered a new job in Switzerland, he decided to take it and move away from us. It hurt so much to think about, so mostly I tried not to.

That's why Mum came up with the crazy idea of moving back to Kira Island, to be near her parents, Mimi and Papa. The only problem was that Mum worked as a stockbroker, and there isn't much work for stockbrokers on a tiny island. So she decided to run a cafe instead. Turns out it wasn't such a mad idea after all.

At first I was ecstatic about getting a puppy. But if I thought it was crowded living in a tiny caravan with my mum, my brother and sister – well, imagine adding a wriggling, bouncing, naughty golden retriever into the mix. Life in our family is never boring!

So what should I do about Mum's mangled shoe? The thought of telling Mum about the fate of her favourite shoes made me feel ill. So I decided to do what any sensible person would do. Hide the evidence! At least for the moment. I hid both shoes (one chewed, one perfect) at the back of the wardrobe, then I crawled around and picked up all the pieces of shredded insole that were scattered all over the floor. These I buried in the bottom of the rubbish bin.

Of course, I'd confess to Mum eventually. I just needed to wait for the right moment. If Mum came home tired and stressed and worried about money then I wouldn't tell her about the shoe until later. If she was happy and relaxed and business had been good – then . . . maybe I wouldn't tell her until later either!

CHAPTER 2

A NEW PROJECT

Early on Monday morning I was walking in the school playground with my friends – Charlie, Meg and Cici. Our school buildings are all white, with pink bougainvillea twisting up the veranda posts and across the roofs. Tall, spreading trees shade the playground. The gardens are filled with lush tropical plants – palms, ferns, jasmine, frangipanis, hibiscus and birds of paradise. It feels more like a jungle than a schoolyard.

The four of us were chatting about our lovely, lazy weekends and my very first surfing lesson. Meg and her brother Jack had taken me to surf with them at Kira Beach. I'd borrowed one of Meg's boards and luckily the waves had been small and gentle. I wasn't very good but it had been fun trying to find my feet on the board.

'Pippa did really well,' said Meg. 'She managed to stand up in her very first lesson.'

'Only once,' I replied. 'I spent most of the time falling off!'

Since I'd grown up in London, I hadn't spent as much time at the beach as my new friends had, but I was loving learning some water sports. Meg particularly loved surfing, sailing, swimming and snorkelling.

'That's normal,' said Charlie. 'It just takes practise. You'll be surfing like a water baby in no time.'

'Meg's the water baby,' I replied. 'She makes it look so easy.'

Meg glowed with pleasure.

'That's because she grew up with dolphins,' joked Cici. She literally had! Meg's mum is a marine biologist studying Kira Island's pod of dolphins. My friends have fascinating lives.

I noticed a poster had been stuck up on the noticeboard outside the library. I stopped to read it.

KIRA COVE CUB REPORTERS

Calling on all year five and six students!

We need keen writers, photographers, artists and designers to help prepare the very first edition of Kira Cove Primary School's student newspaper.

Our first meeting will be in the library at lunchtime on Monday.

Prizes will be awarded for the best stories.

It will be fantastic! Looking forward to seeing you there.

Mrs Neill

'Look at this,' I said. 'Wouldn't it be fun? I'd love to write some stories for the school newspaper.'

'What's a *cub* reporter?' asked Charlie.

'It's a young trainee journalist,' I replied. 'I saw a movie once set in a magazine office in New York. The cub reporters were always on the prowl trying to unearth amazing scoops.'

'I'm not much of a writer,' said Meg.

'No, but you're a fantastic photographer,' said Charlie. 'And you have excellent ideas.'

Cici laughed. 'Between the four of us we cover everything — writers, photographers, artists and designers. We could do the whole newspaper on our own!'

Cici was right. I loved writing, drawing and designing. Charlie was fantastic at art and graphic design, just like her mother. Meg was a wonderful photographer and clever at research. And Cici was a great stylist and very organised. We'd be a perfect newspaper team.

'We should at least go along to the meeting and find out what it's all about,' said Charlie.

'Let's do it,' said Meg.

So that's how we found ourselves in the library at lunchtime, sprawling on beanbags, chatting with the other kids and waiting for our librarian, Mrs Neill, to tell us all about the project.

The library is my favourite place at school. It has lots of cosy nooks for reading and lounging, shelves lined with hundreds of books, and colourful artwork on the walls. When I first came to Kira Cove School, it was a refuge when I felt sad. Now it felt like my home away from home.

A few latecomers straggled in and took their places. There were now about twenty students, a mixture of boys and girls from years five and six.

'Thank you for coming, everyone,' announced Mrs Neill. 'Our principal has had the wonderful idea of launching a school newspaper run by our pupils. Our student volunteers will come up with ideas for stories, take photographs, cover sporting events, interview interesting people and report on newsworthy events around the school and our local community.'

I felt a buzz of excitement. Writing for the school newspaper definitely sounded like fun.

'The newspaper will be published fortnightly, but the first issue will probably take the most work,' explained Mrs Neill. 'We have two weeks to research, write and edit the stories ready for publication. I'm assigning the year six students as editors – they will decide which stories go in the paper, where they go on each page, and whether stories should be kept for later issues.'

A group of year six students started whispering among themselves. I noticed Meg's brother, Jack, as well as Charlie's stepbrother Seb. Jack was jotting in a notebook.

Mrs Neill waited until everyone was quiet again. 'Don't forget that each story is a lot of work. It needs to be researched, written, photographed or illustrated, edited and laid out for our newspaper before the deadline. While we can meet every Monday and Thursday at lunchtime in the library to work on the project, you might also need to spend some time on the weekends and after school.'

A couple of the kids didn't look quite so keen when they realised it would involve extra time out of school hours.

'I'll be here if you need any guidance, but the idea is that this is a newspaper for the students, by the students,' continued Mrs Neill. 'So, can I please see a show of hands from those students who would like to be involved?'

I shot my hand up into the air, as did most of the other kids in the room.

'Fantastic to see everyone so keen,' said Mrs Neill. 'Does anyone have any questions?'

There were lots of questions judging by the number of raised hands.

'Yes, Pippa?' asked Mrs Neill.

'Can we work on stories in a group?' I asked. 'Or do we need to do one individually?'

'You can choose if you would like to do your own story or work as a team,' she replied.

Cici, Meg, Charlie and I grinned at each other. The Sassy Sisters would definitely make a brilliant team.

'How many pages will we need to fill?' asked Seb.

'I'm hoping the first issue will be about ten pages,' replied Mrs Neill. 'So we'll need a mix of short and longer stories. That's roughly half a page per student or two pages for a group of four.'

There were a number of other questions from students. A year six girl asked about what type of stories could be written.

'Think about what stories you'd like to report

on, then check in with the year six editors to make sure we have a good spread of stories and no doubling up,' suggested Mrs Neill. 'I'm sure there are a lot of students who'd love to cover the Friday sport results!'

There were a few giggles and another bout of eager chatter.

'Okay, let's get to work,' said Mrs Neill. She went to talk to the year six students about how the editing process would work.

Charlie, Cici, Meg and I huddled in a corner in deep discussion.

We weren't the only ones who decided to work as a team. Some of the year five boys – Alex, Rory, Sam and Joey – formed another group. From overhearing their excited conversation, they were all dead keen on writing a collection of short stories on different sports. There were also two year six teams, as well as a few kids who preferred to work on their own.

Across the room I could see Olivia Gray. She was with a group of girls including Sienna, Tash and Willow. They were being very secretive and whispering madly. Olivia is my arch rival at school. While initially we had been friendly, Olivia and I always seem to end up competing with each other. For the last couple of weeks we had been getting on fairly well, but I could never be sure when she might turn on me. I was glad Olivia wasn't on our team.

The different groups clustered together chatting and giggling. Everyone sounded like they had tons of ideas.

I felt a thrill of excitement. What fantastic idea could we come up with for our story? Perhaps we'd get our names printed in the newspaper? Wouldn't that be brilliant!

CHAPTER 3

SQUABBLING

Our group began by tossing around ideas for stories we'd like to work on. Meg and I were given the job of jotting down notes.

Our first thoughts weren't so great but then we all started making suggestions that sounded more promising.

'We should have a guessing competition where we get baby photos from the teachers and everyone has to guess which baby is which teacher,' said Charlie. 'That would be hilarious.'

No one else looked overly keen on that one.

'How about a story on our Friday afternoon kayaking and sailing?' said Meg. 'That's always lots of fun. Or maybe we could cover some of the Saturday touch football games.'

'No. I bet Mrs Neill is right about lots of kids wanting to write sport stories,' said Cici. 'We need to come up with something totally amazing and original.'

'How about interviewing interesting people from the local community?' I suggested. 'You know our prickly neighbour, Mrs Beecham? She was once a world famous ballet dancer. She must have some incredible stories.'

'Mmm . . . maybe,' said Cici.

'I like that idea,' said Charlie. 'But perhaps we could interview kids about what they want to be when they grow up. We could do lots of short interviews with different kids.'

Meg and I scribbled that one down. Of course, my notes were decorated with endless doodles. A pod of dolphins cavorted in waves down the margin of my notebook.

'We could ask them what their hobbies are,' I said. 'Or interview them and find out what they would do if they were principal for a day. That would be funny.'

'I'd love to run the school! I'd make longer breaks so we had more play time,' said Cici. 'And start school later so we could sleep in.'

'I'd ban maths forever and make a rule that every class had its own special pet,' said Charlie. 'Then I'd order the canteen to serve free party food to all the kids at lunchtime.'

We all giggled at the thought.

I scribbled down the ideas. 'We could do a whole two pages just on that!'

Cici leaned forward.

'Actually, what I think we should do is a really cool fashion shoot,' said Cici. 'We could choose some gorgeous clothes and accessories, and photograph kids modelling them down at the beach.'

Cici's mum was a well-known fashion designer, so Cici knew a lot about fashion.

'That would be awesome,' agreed Charlie. 'We'd easily get enough photos to do a two-page spread.'

Meg chewed the end of her pen while she thought. 'A fashion shoot would be fun but I think this is a perfect opportunity to do something important. I'd love to write about an environmental issue like endangered animals or pollution.'

Meg looked super-serious – or, as Cici liked to say, she had her 'Wildlife Warrior' face on. Meg had grown up living on a marine animal research yacht and she was passionate about protecting all kinds of endangered animals.

In fact, it had been Meg's love for threatened African animals such as rhinos, lions and ele-phants that had helped us to win equal first in the school science competition. The four of us had made a 3D board game with models of African animals that were in danger of becoming extinct. We were all very excited about representing our school at the regional science competition on the mainland in a few weeks.

'Well, we've come up with some really great ideas,' I said. 'But as Mrs Neill said, it is going to be a lot of work so perhaps we should vote to do one of them.'

'The fashion shoot,' said Cici adamantly.

Meg looked mutinous and crossed her arms. 'Fashion is frivolous, but saving endangered wildlife is really important.'

'But we just made the Wildlife Warrior game,' pleaded Cici. 'And the fashion shoot will be so much fun . . . Pretty pleeease?'

'They're both good ideas, but I still like the idea of interviewing kids the best,' said Charlie, throwing her blonde plait over her shoulder. 'What kids want to do when they grow up, or some fun questions like what their favourite ice-cream flavour is.'

'Salted caramel,' said Cici at once.

'No! Chocolate all the way!' retorted Charlie.

This was hopeless.

'Come on, guys,' I said. 'Ice-cream is a little off topic!'

Meg huffed with annoyance. 'And, as usual, totally silly! But you can do whatever you like. *I'm* writing about rhinos.'

'Kids don't want to read about rhinos,' retorted Cici. 'They want to read about cool things like fashion, celebrities and funny people.'

Meg looked really hurt. 'Not all kids are totally trivial.'

My heart sank. This was not what I had imagined. The four of us were squabbling over ideas before we'd even started. This was meant to be fun!

We discussed all the ideas some more. The problem was that everyone liked their own ideas the best so we reached a stalemate. It looked like it would be my job to be the negotiator so we could reach some sort of compromise.

'They're all *brilliant* ideas,' I said. 'But we need to decide if we want to work together as a team on one story, or go our separate ways and do our own stories.'

Everyone thought for a few moments. Meg still had her arms crossed, looking very stubborn.

'The fashion shoot will be too hard to do on my own,' admitted Cici. 'We need to source lots of different clothes and I need you all to model. Plus we'd need a photographer, a writer, a layout designer and a stylist so it means we can all do something that we're good at.'

'It would be great to do something together,' said Charlie. 'It could be a Sassy Sisters club project.'

'Well, I like the idea of interviewing kids or someone interesting from the community,' I said. 'But I think the two best ideas for the first issue are the fashion shoot or Meg's environment story. So why don't we vote?'

Meg, of course, voted for wildlife. Cici and Charlie voted for fashion. So it was up to me to make the deciding vote.

'I'm so sorry, Meg,' I said, looking at her with sympathy. 'I'm voting for the fashion shoot. I love your wildlife story idea, but perhaps we can do it next time? I really want to do this together as a team.'

Meg looked upset for a moment. Charlie gave her a hug.

'Cheer up, Megs,' said Cici. 'You can't be a wildlife warrior all the time. It'll be fun, I promise.'

Meg sighed, then she smiled at us all. 'Of course I want to do the story with you guys. We wouldn't be the Sassy Sisters without me!'

I was happy that Meg had decided to come around. I hated it when we squabbled over silly stuff.

Just then, the bell rang for the end of lunch.

'We didn't get very far,' said Charlie.

'But at least we know what we're going to do now,' I said.

'How about we have a club meeting after school this afternoon?' suggested Cici. 'At the Beach Shack?'

My heart warmed. 'Absolutely.'

CHAPTER 4

CLUB MEETING

As planned, Charlie, Meg, Cici and I had our Sassy Sisters club meeting after school to organise our newspaper story.

For once I didn't have to walk my brother and sister to the boatshed. Harry was practising his new passion, playing touch football in the playground. In London, he'd loved football, and now that he'd joined the school touch football team he was keen to hone his skills. Bella had been picked up by one of her friends' parents to play. So it was just the four of us, walking together to the Beach Shack.

When we arrived the cafe was buzzing with people. The tables and chairs out on the jetty were also filled with cheerful customers. Zoe, our red-haired barista, waved to us from behind the coffee machine as she made a series of lattes, espressos and cappuccinos with love hearts, butterflies and flowers in the froth. Zoe was a whiz at latte art. It was a lot like doodling only using coffee and milk.

A group of kids were there in their school uniforms ordering afternoon tea. I was thrilled to see that the cupcakes, made to Cici's family recipe, were super-popular. Our specialties were zingy lemon, mango-and-coconut, chocaholic and pink vanilla.

My personal favourite were Cici's pupcakes, which were decorated with the cutest puppy faces, but they were far too much work for the everyday cafe menu. We also sold mini berry cheesecakes, French lemon tartlets, and choc-chunk cookies. Of course, Mum made sure there were lots of healthy options too, like tropical-fruit kebabs, frozen yoghurt lollipops, and a mezze plate with hummus and veggie sticks.

Mum was serving behind the counter, making up a three-tiered stand with a mixture of different cupcakes, fresh strawberries and chicken-and-lettuce finger sandwiches. The Beach Shack high tea special had proven to be a hit.

'Hello, girls,' said Mum as she saw us come in. 'Why don't you take a seat wherever you can find one and I'll get you something to eat.'

My favourite spot was a little round table in the corner near the window with views out to sea. Zoe always made sure it was kept free for us to use after school. We sat down and began talking about Cici's idea for the fashion shoot. She had printed off some beachy photos from different websites to give us some ideas.

In a couple of minutes, Zoe came over with

a tray laden with four creamy, ice-cold mango smoothies, a plate of fruit kebabs and four zingy lemon cupcakes.

'Thanks so much, Zoe,' we all chorused.

'Pleasure, girls. Lovely to see you,' said Zoe. She pushed an escaped red curl back behind her ear.

'How's your new job going, Zoe?' Meg asked.

Zoe beamed. 'Fantastic. I love working here with Pippa's mum. The customers are chatty and friendly, and I get to go for a swim or a surf in my breaks. I've even joined the Kira surf lifesaving club and started doing volunteer patrols on Tuesday and Sunday afternoons. It's so much fun.'

Zoe was staying at Kira Island for a working holiday before she started university. She was bright and bubbly, and the customers loved her. She had even managed to charm our crotchety neighbour, Mrs Beecham. It had taken me a lot longer to get on Mrs B's good side.

I saw Mrs Beecham sitting at a nearby table, sipping tea with one of the other regulars. I waved to her and she waved back with a friendly smile.

Zoe peered at the photos that Cici had spread out over the table. 'Love those clothes, Cici. Are they your mum's designs?' There was floral beachwear, T-shirts with cut-off jeans, sporting gear and tutu-inspired party dresses.

'No,' said Cici. 'These are some ideas for a fashion photo shoot we're planning for our school newspaper. We want lots of gorgeous summer styles for boys and girls.'

'Sounds like fun,' said Zoe. 'Let me know if I can help in any way.'

Zoe bustled off to look after the next customers. Meg, Cici and I helped ourselves to a fruit kebab – a bamboo skewer of pineapple, banana, strawberries and mango. Charlie broke off a piece of cake and nibbled it. .

'Your mum is really getting the hang of baking these cupcakes,' said Charlie.

'Do you remember the first afternoon tea we had here before the Beach Shack opened?' said Cici.

I grimaced. 'How could I forget? Green gloop and sawdust muffins,' I joked. Mum had made, of all things, a seaweed and broccoli smoothie for us to try. It was so terrible we fed it all to the fish!

The mango smoothies, however, were delicious and my new favourite afternoon treat.

'How's the adorable Summer, Pippa?' asked Charlie. 'I can't wait to see her again.'

I shuddered theatrically. 'You mean *wicked* Summer? She's absolutely loveable. But she is *so* naughty! I haven't had the heart to tell Mum that Summer ate one of her favourite shoes.'

'Oh *noooo*,' said Cici, her dark eyes twinkling. 'Not the shoes! Your mum won't be happy about that. When can you bring her out for walks?'

'Not until she's had all her injections,' I explained. 'She's ten weeks old now so another few weeks.'

'I can't wait to introduce her to Zorro and Bandit,' said Charlie. 'We can take them to the park to rumble together.'

Charlie loves dogs and animals of all kinds. Her family have lots of pets, including two donkeys called Archie and Clementine, five chickens, a cat called Trixie, and a lamb called Maisie. But her favourites are her two black-and-white border collies. Both dogs have black masks across their eyes that make them look a bit like robbers, which is why they are called Bandit and Zorro.

'Muffin would love that too,' added Cici. Her dog is a little puggle – half beagle, half pug and very cute. 'They can form their own little pooch club.'

'I don't think Neptune would enjoy that club very much,' said Meg. 'He hates dogs.'

I giggled at the thought of Meg's aloof ship's cat trying to make friends with all the wild and playful dogs bounding in the park.

'Maybe having some doggy friends will teach Summer some manners,' I said. 'I'm trying to teach her to behave but she's not very obedient yet.'

'I'll help you train her,' offered Charlie. 'I can come around one afternoon and show you some tricks.'

'That would be perfect,' I said. 'Imagine how thrilled Mum would be if I could teach Summer not to chew everything in sight!'

'Look who's here,' said Cici, glancing over to the counter. There was a group of girls from school – Willow, Sienna, Tash and Olivia. All the girls had come to the launch party two weeks ago. Willow and Sienna had been to the cafe a few times now. Willow's mum was talking to my mum.

I felt proud to see so many kids from school visiting our cafe. This was exactly what we'd hoped for. It looked like the cafe was doing well.

Most of the girls were chatting and laughing. Olivia stared around taking in the atmosphere.

To me the cafe looked gorgeous. There was a bookshop area with comfy sofas and armchairs. A long window seat ran along the left wall, with feather cushions and stunning views of the cove. All the little tables were crowded with customers chatting over their drinks, so too was the long refectory table that ran down the centre of the room.

Mum decorated the space with dozens of iron buckets overflowing with bunches of fresh flowers every week. Today there was a profusion of hot-pink and orange with a pop of summery blue.

I remembered back to when I first arrived at Kira Cove School. Olivia had told me that her father said that some idiot had paid a ridiculous amount of money for a falling-down old shack. In a funny way, this was what inspired the name the Beach Shack. I wonder what she'd think if she knew?

CHAPTER 5

A SPECIAL SECRET

Willow's mum led the group of girls past our table. They were heading outside to the jetty where there were more tables and chairs. We all waved and called out hellos.

I noticed that Cici quickly packed up her collection of photos and slid them away in her bag.

Willow paused beside us, looking curious. The others crowded around behind her.

'Are you guys working on your story for the newspaper?' she asked.

'Yes,' said Charlie. 'We're going to –'

Cici quickly interrupted her. 'We're still trying to decide what we're going to do.'

'That's what we're doing here too,' said Sienna. 'A brainstorming session!'

'Jack said that they're looking for a really catchy story to go on the front page with a big photo,' added Olivia. 'Something really different or unusual. That's our mission!'

I felt a prickle of doubt. We hadn't thought of writing a story especially for the front cover. Was the photo shoot idea catchy enough? Probably not. Could we make it more interesting?

'Have you come up with any ideas yet?' asked Meg.

Olivia, Willow, Sienna and Tash grinned as though they were hiding a special secret.

'You bet,' said Tash, sounding mysterious. 'Something really cool.'

'We've come up with an absolutely *amazing* idea,' said Olivia. Her blue eyes sparkled with excitement. 'But we can't say anything until it's definite. We don't want to jinx it.'

'Can't you give us even a tiny hint?' asked Cici. 'Otherwise we might be working on the same idea.'

'I doubt that,' said Olivia, rather smugly, I thought. 'We'll let you know once it's all confirmed.'

Charlie, Meg, Cici and I looked at each other in frustration. I was burning up with curiosity. What could those girls be planning?

'It sounds exciting,' I said. 'Good luck with it.'

The girls said goodbye and hurried outside, almost skipping with anticipation.

'I wonder what brilliant idea they've come up with?' I asked. I must admit I felt just a twinge of jealousy.

'Don't worry about their story,' said Charlie. 'Let's get on with ours! We voted to do the photo shoot so let's get planning.'

'What did you have in mind, Cici?' asked Meg, picking up her pen.

Cici leaned forward, her face alight with enthusiasm. 'I want to show a range of beautiful but affordable clothes for kids our age, both girls and boys. Everything from swim and beachwear, sports and casual gear, to the hottest new looks for parties, with ideas on how to style the look.'

'That sounds great,' said Meg. 'I hate looking at magazines and reading that the T-shirt I like costs a small fortune.'

'How will we get the clothes?' I asked. 'Will kids just wear their own things from home?'

Cici shook her head, her dark hair swinging. 'When Mum worked as a stylist on a fashion magazine, they would borrow the clothes from different stores and return them afterwards. So I'm sure the little shops around town would be happy to lend us some things if we're careful with them.'

Meg and I scribbled down notes.

'So we take the photos at the beach,' Charlie said. 'But we need to make the photos really beautiful.'

'Yes, and sassy,' said Cici. 'We don't want stiff, awkward shots of kids standing still like in the department store catalogue. We should take photos of kids doing stuff they really love doing. Like Charlie being a boho-mermaid playing her guitar on the rocks. Or Meg looking sporty and gorgeous with her surfboard.'

'Or Pippa cuddling her adorable puppy, all wild-haired and gypsy-like,' added Charlie. 'And Cici bossing all of us around!'

'Exactly,' said Cici with a cheeky grin. 'Our very favourite activities!'

This was more like it. This was fun. The Sassy Sisters working together as a team.

'I can borrow my mum's camera to take the photos,' said Meg, jotting herself a reminder. 'I'm sure she won't mind.'

'And we need someone else to take photos as well, so that Meg can be in some of them,' said Cici. 'The more we have the better.'

'I can try if Meg shows me what to do,' I said. 'I might be able to borrow Mum's camera too.' I glanced over to where Mum was working behind the counter.

'Easy,' said Meg. 'I'll teach you.'

So the four of us set to work on planning our story and making lists of what we needed to do. Meg and Charlie searched for photos on the internet. Cici made a list of shops on the island that we could ask. I jotted down ideas as we came up with them.

This is what my notes looked like:

Sassy Sisters Photo Shoot

- Photo shoot at the beach - palm trees, boulders, bicycle on the esplanade, rock pool, running on the sand, sunset for that Kira Island glow.

- Kids doing what they love - playing guitar, surfing, swimming, playing with puppy, dancing, singing, riding a bike, kicking a ball, picnic, skateboarding.
- Clothes - swimming costumes, beachwear, casual clothes for mucking about, party clothes, accessories, shoes.
- Models - Meg, Charlie, Pippa, Cici, Alex, Sam, Joey and Rory (ask boys if they are happy to help).
- Stylists - Cici and Charlie.
- Photographer - Meg with Pippa as assistant. Beautiful arty photos, with interesting angles and golden light.
- Copy writer - Pippa and Cici.
- Caterer - Cici to bake cupcakes to bribe models and shop owners. Beg Pippa's mum to use the Beach Shack.
- Layout design for article - Charlie.

To do:

- Ask boys to be models.
- Source clothes from local shops (beach, casual and party).
- Borrow Meg's mum's camera.
- Organise photo shoot for this Saturday.
- Ask my mum if we can use the Beach Shack as a base for the photo shoot (change room, storage, snacks!).
- Bake cupcakes.
- Dress and style models.
- Take photos.
- Let shops share photos for their own advertising (bribery!).
- Write captions and story on Sunday.
- Design layout.
- Edit and submit to year six next Monday – phew!!!

We had a plan. Now we just had to make it happen.

CHAPTER 6

MY NEW JOB

'How's upstairs coming along?' asked Cici. The girls, especially Cici, all loved checking on the progress of our renovation. It was like magic, watching the dusty, tumbledown old shack being transformed.

Our builders, Jason, Dan and Miguel, had managed to get the downstairs of the boatshed finished in time for the cafe to open two weeks ago, but they still had loads of work to do to get the upper storey finished. Upstairs was going to be where we would eventually live.

'Why don't we take a look?' I suggested.

We all cleared our notebooks and Mum's laptop off the table and carried our glasses and plates to the kitchen bench to save Zoe from having to do it. Then we climbed the stairs.

The huge old attic had been divided into rooms to make an apartment for us. At first, I was worried that Mum was going to make us live in a dusty attic with holes in the floor. But all the rooms had walls now and you could almost see how the finished flat would look.

At one end, the living area and kitchen had floor-to-ceiling glass doors, which opened onto a balcony with glorious views of the cove. At the other end were Bella and Harry's rooms, which faced towards the shore and the olive-green mountains behind the village. In the middle were my room and Mum's room. I led the girls into the living room, where the builders were just packing up their tools.

'Hello, girls,' said Dan, as he took his tool belt off and put it away in a large chest. 'Did you bring any of those delicious cupcakes up with you?'

'No, sorry,' I said, feeling rather guilty. All three of the builders loved sweet treats and they had worked so hard to help us that we liked to spoil them. 'I can run down and fetch something if you like?'

Jason pretended to cuff Dan over the head. 'That's all right, Pippa. Don't you dare! Dan's just trying to trick you. Your mum brought us up some choc-chunk cookies only an hour ago.'

Dan laughed. 'Well, it was worth a try.'

The girls and I looked around to see what had been done since we were last up here. The builders were working on framing up some cupboards in the kitchen.

'Have you come to check on our progress?' asked Jason. We all nodded. 'Well, we've been working mostly in here this week, but there's also a little surprise in your bedroom that you might want to check out.'

'What have you done in my room?' I asked.

Jason picked up his backpack, with a wide grin. 'It wouldn't be a surprise if I told you, would it? See you later, girls. Enjoy.'

Miguel and Dan said goodbye as well and they all headed off.

The girls and I rushed into my new bedroom. It was small and empty, but it had a wide window with views up the beach and out to sea. It took me a moment to work out what was different. Then I saw it beside the window.

I pulled open the door of my new cupboard. There weren't any shelves or drawers inside yet, but there was the narrow ladder that led up to my secret tower room.

'They've built some cupboards,' I said, brimming with enthusiasm. 'And they've hidden the ladder inside!'

'No one will know how to get up there,' said Charlie with glee. 'Unless you tell them.'

Of course, we had to climb up immediately.

The tower room was perfectly round with views in all directions. It was still empty and dirty, with salt-smeared windows and cobwebs in the corners. But eventually it would be a secret space where our club could meet and hang out.

'How are you going to decorate up here?' asked Cici. We all looked around.

'I'm not sure,' I said. 'I want to make it really special, but I'm not sure exactly how.'

'It already is special,' said Meg.

Cici had a dreamy expression on her face.

'Maybe a velvety rug on the floor and piles of brightly coloured cushions,' she suggested. 'And floaty curtains at the window.'

Cici always had fabulous fashion and styling ideas.

'Perfect,' I agreed. 'And a bookshelf, of course!'

'It will need to be a round bookshelf,' said Charlie. 'To fit the round wall.'

We chatted for a while longer and then we climbed back down the ladder.

'And what about down here?' Cici ran a finger along the unpainted wall. 'Have you decided on paint colours and furniture?'

I shook my head. 'I'm not sure. I've thought about it loads but there's just so much to choose from.'

'Turquoise would be gorgeous,' said Charlie. 'Or an apple-green.'

'What you need to do is to create a mood board,' said Cici decisively. 'You know like the one on the wall of my mum's studio?'

I remembered that Nathalie's studio had a large black board on one wall which was covered in fashion photographs, design sketches and swatches of material.

'It's just like my lookbook or your mum's ideas folio,' explained Cici. 'You search for

51

photos of rooms on the internet or in mag-azines. Then you stick up the photos of all your favourite rooms and ideas. It will help you decide what look you love the most.'

It made sense. 'Thanks, Cici. I'll give it a go.'

I felt a fizzing of excitement. Only a few more weeks of living in the caravan and then our new home would be ready to move into.

'I'd better get home,' said Meg, checking her watch.

'Me too,' said Charlie.

So we all clattered down the stairs together, then the girls said goodbye and left.

'There you are, Pipkin,' said Mum. 'Could you come and give me a hand, please?'

The cafe was nearly empty now. There were just a few tables occupied outside. A busi-nessman was sitting out on the jetty working on his laptop. A couple of mums were chatting, with their babies in prams beside them.

Nearly every table was covered in dirty crockery, teapots, milk jugs, glasses, water bottles, cake stands, and crumpled paper napkins. The place was a total mess! Zoe was cleaning the coffee machine while Mum was sitting at the long table with piles of dockets and order forms.

'I was wondering if you'd like to earn some pocket money?' asked Mum.

A joyous vision came to me of having spending money. I could buy some art supplies or go to the movies. Perhaps I could save up to buy some summer clothes. Money had been very tight in our family for the last few months so I hadn't had anything new for ages.

'Absolutely,' I replied.

'Great,' said Mum. 'Why don't you clear all the tables and wipe them down? Then you can pack the dishwasher while I tally up the receipts and check the cash register.'

My heart sank as I looked at the terrible

mess. It would take ages! I decided to focus on one table at a time.

I set to work. One by one I cleared each table, carrying all the dirty crockery into the kitchen, rinsing and stacking everything by the sink and throwing the rubbish into the bin. Then every table had to be wiped down so there was not a crumb or a smear or a grain of sugar. Zoe made me redo the first couple because they weren't quite perfect!

Next, I had to empty the dishwasher, stacking all the cups, saucers and plates neatly. I wasn't sure where everything went. Lastly, I had to pack the dishwasher with the dirty dishes. Zoe made me restack the dishes, making sure that they weren't too close together or taking up too much room.

The last customers paid and left, and Mum finally locked the front door and the sliding windows leading out to the jetty. Then Zoe had to vacuum and mop the floors. It was a big job to get everything ready for the next day. Mum filed the receipts and came to help me finish cleaning the kitchen. At last we were done. Mum and Zoe hung up their aprons and we went outside.

It was a beautiful time of day on Kira Island with the sun sinking in the west and the island bathed in a golden light. As we walked along the beachfront, Mum handed me a precious ten-dollar note.

'Great work today, Pipkin,' said Mum. 'I really appreciated your help.'

'Thanks, Mum,' I said, as I tucked my money away safely in my pocket. I wandered along, dreaming of all the things I could save for.

A group of girls ran past on their way back from the beach. All of them were wearing swimming costumes in pretty tropical colours.

That reminded me of how Olivia had sneered at my boring old navy one.

That's what I would save for! A gorgeous

new swimming costume. It would take a lot of afternoons helping at the cafe, but it would be something I would use all the time. And boy, did I need one!

CHAPTER 7

SURF LESSON

Meg and I had made plans for Tuesday afternoon. Meg and her brother, Jack, had promised me another surf lesson at the beach. I was super-excited about learning to surf because after years of living in central London, we now lived a stone's throw from one of the most stunning beaches in the world.

I hurried Bella and Harry out of the playground in double-quick time and marched them to the Beach Shack. Mum stopped work to kiss us all and ask a few quick questions about our day. I zipped into the storeroom to change into my despised navy-blue swimming costume, with shorts and a T-shirt over the top.

Then I was racing up the esplanade towards the surf beach to meet the others. The village of Kira Cove is built in a sheltered bay at the southern end of the island. Heading north, the surf beach opens to the ocean with a long paved esplanade and a grassy parkland running alongside.

Kids dashed back and forth on scooters, bikes and skateboards. A group of young mums were doing a kickboxing class under the palm trees, while their toddlers played ring-a-rosie. Surfers in black wetsuits jogged past as sleek as seals.

'Hey, Pippa. Over here.' Meg waved madly at me.

Meg and Jack were waiting for me with their mum, Mariana. They were all sitting on the stone seawall near the Kira surf life-saving club in the afternoon sunshine. A flock of grey-haired older people were practising tai chi on the sand, their movements like a courtly dance.

'It's a gorgeous afternoon for a surfing lesson, Pippa,' said Mariana, with a welcoming smile. 'The waves are perfect for a beginner.'

'Let's go!' said Jack, grabbing his board and doing up his leg-rope. 'It's time to hit the water!'

Mariana sat on her towel and watched us, waving from the shore. Meg had brought me a spare beginner surfboard to borrow. As we jogged down the sand carrying our boards, Jack paused to scan the ocean. Meg and I stopped too.

'Make sure you stay inside the flags, Pippa,' said Jack, waving to the left.

The red-and-yellow patrol flags fluttered in the breeze, marking where it was safe to swim. Four lifesavers in red-and-yellow striped caps and shirts stood on guard watching the swimmers. As a beginner, I could practise surfing there. However, the more experienced surfers like Meg and Jack had to surf further down the beach.

Jack pointed down the beach to the right. 'There's a rip running out to sea down there, so make sure you stay well away from it.'

I peered at the spot in the ocean that Jack had indicated. To my inexperienced eye the surf there looked the same as along the rest of the beach. The waves peeled gently onto the beach, foaming on the sand. Sunlight dazzled off the water.

'How can you tell?' I asked. 'I can't see anything different.'

'Don't worry,' said Jack. 'Most mainlanders can't see rips, but now that you live here on the island, it's important you learn how to spot them.'

'Can you see that the water in that patch has

less waves breaking?' asked Meg. 'Where the sea is cloudy and sandy?'

'Yes,' I replied, noticing that a rectangle of water looked slightly flatter, with waves foaming on either side.

'Waves aren't breaking there because there is a strong current sucking the water and sand back out to sea,' explained Meg. 'If you get caught there, you'll get dragged out with it.'

I felt a shiver run down my spine. The sea around Kira Island looked so beautiful, but Mimi and Papa had warned me that it could be dangerous.

'That sounds scary,' I said. 'I don't want to get sucked out to sea and lost forever!'

'You'll be safe between the flags,' Jack assured me. 'And if you do get into trouble, make sure you put your arm straight up in the air as a signal to the lifesavers. Have fun!' He waved goodbye and jogged down the beach past the rip to safer waters.

Meg and I walked towards the patrol flags. One of the surf lifesavers noticed us and waved.

'Hi, Pippa, hi, Meg,' she called.

I took a second look and realised that it was Zoe, our bubbly red-haired barista.

'Hi, Zoe,' we chorused.

Zoe introduced us to her patrol captain, Nigel, an older man who looked super-fit and strong from years of swimming and running. He watched the swimmers while Zoe chatted to us about our day. The other two lifesavers were stationed further down the beach.

'How's the surfing coming along, Pippa?' asked Zoe.

'Slowly,' I replied. 'It's harder than I thought. Meg makes it look so easy.'

'It just takes *lots* of time in the water,' said Zoe. 'You'll get the hang of it.'

I rolled my eyes. 'That's what Meg says!'

Meg laughed. 'And I'm right! Come on, land-lubber. Let's do it!'

Just like on Sunday, Meg made me practise 'paddling' on the beach. I lay down on the board while it rested on the sand, then jumped to my feet in a crouched position, left foot forward. We did this a few times together until I could jump up quite easily.

Then Meg and I splashed out into the water between the flags. Meg left her board on the sand so that she could wade out with me to give me tips, push me onto waves and encourage me.

For the first few waves I was, as I feared, pretty hopeless. Most times I couldn't even get to my feet. Then I managed to crouch and eventually stand before being bucked off by the wave and slipping into the sea.

There were a few other people swimming nearby. I hoped there weren't any kids from my school. I didn't really want anyone I knew to see how dreadful I was. Meg smiled encouragingly as though reading my mind.

'You're getting better, I promise you.'

At last, a few minutes before it was time to go, I jumped to my feet and rode a wave all the way to the sand. 'Woohoo,' I shouted, giddy with exhilaration. 'That was incredible.'

'You did it,' cried Meg. 'We'll make a surfer out of you yet!'

CHAPTER 8

THE NAUGHTIEST PUPPY IN THE WORLD

Afterwards, I met Mum, Bella and Harry and we walked home together from the beach.

Mum sent me to collect Summer from Mimi and Papa's cottage. Mimi minds Summer during the day while we're at school and Mum is at work. I knocked on the back door and went inside.

'Summer, Summer,' I called. A streak of gold and white came tearing towards me. Then I realised that Summer was trailing a long white tail.

'Oh, Summer, what have you done?' I asked.
'You naughty puppy!'

Summer had the end of a roll of toilet paper in her mouth. The whole roll had been pulled from the bathroom all around the house in a twisted trail. Summer dashed away again, rolling over and over, knotting herself in the toilet paper. She was having a wonderful time with her new toy.

I gave chase but the faster I followed the faster Summer ran. The toilet roll unfurled even further. Summer dashed under the couch, between the dining chairs and to her basket in the kitchen. She dived headfirst into the cushion and rolled over, giving up the chase. She lay on her back, with four paws in the air, looking up at me with huge, soft, brown eyes. She smiled at me, her pink tongue lolling. My heart melted.

'I can't get cross with you,' I complained. 'Even though you are the naughtiest puppy on the planet.'

Just then Mimi came in. She was all dressed up, ready to go out with Papa to meet friends.

'Hello, darling Pippa,' she said. 'And what mischief has Miss Summer been up to while I was gone for three minutes?'

I sighed as I scrabbled about trying to gather up the metres of tangled toilet paper.

'I'm so sorry, Mimi,' I said. 'But Summer has made a mega-mess and destroyed a roll of toilet paper.'

Mimi laughed. 'Another one? That's the third roll this week. But it's my fault for leaving the bathroom door open.'

'She's *soooo* naughty,' I grumbled, as I stuffed an armful of paper in the recycling bin. 'I never thought that having a puppy would be so much trouble.'

'She's just a baby,' said Mimi. 'She'll learn. You just need to be firm with her and teach her a few basic commands.'

Mimi leaned down to stroke Summer on the forehead. 'Plus, it helps if you use your human brain to think about what mischief she might get into and remove the temptation,' she said. 'For example, from now on I'll be keeping the bathroom door closed and, just to be safe, I'll put the loo roll on top of the bathroom cabinet rather than hanging it where Summer can reach it.'

That made sense. We had never had a dog before. Mum had grown up with dogs when she was a child, but in London she had always said we needed to wait until we were older, or had a bigger garden, or she had more time to look after it. To be honest, I think the truth was that my dad had never really liked the idea of getting a dog. I think I was beginning to see why!

As always, the thought of Dad made me feel sad and hollow inside. I quickly picked up Summer and gave her a tight cuddle.

'How do I train her to be good?' I asked. Summer snuggled in, then squirmed in protest. I put her down at my feet.

Mimi opened the container of puppy food that was on the bench. She took out a few pieces of kibble.

'This is what I do during the day when I feed her,' said Mimi. 'She's a really fast learner and keen to please, so she'll be easy to train.'

Mimi held out her hand so Summer could see and smell the food. Mimi stepped away a few metres.

'Summer, come,' commanded Mimi.

Obediently, Summer raced to Mimi's feet. I scooped out more loo paper from her basket.

'Summer, sit.' Mimi pointed her hand downwards.

Summer plopped down on her chubby haunches, her tongue lolling with anticipation.

Mimi held out her hand in a stop motion. 'Summer, *staaay.*'

Mimi put two pieces of kibble in Summer's bowl. Summer strained towards the bowl, her bottom sliding a few centimetres across the floor, but she stayed more or less sitting.

'Good girl, Summer!' The puppy bounded across the floor to her bowl and gulped down the kibble in one second flat. Mimi rubbed her all over her back and tummy.

'Now you try, Pippa,' suggested Mimi, handing me a couple more pieces of kibble. 'Go and stand over there.'

So I repeated all the commands. Summer had clearly decided that I was not the boss because she refused to do anything I told her. But then Mimi made me show her the food, and do it all again, making sure my voice was firm, and my hand movements strong. This time Summer obeyed until I put the food in the bowl. She dashed straight for it, her tail wagging madly.

'Pick up the bowl, Pippa,' said Mimi. 'Don't let her eat unless she does the right thing.

And make sure that you never feed Summer without making her run through all these commands.'

I grabbed the bowl. Summer hopefully licked the floor where the bowl had been as though it might magically reappear.

'Now do it all again,' said Mimi. 'She'll soon learn that she will only get food if she comes, sits and *stays* on command. And then she'll learn the meaning of the words so that she'll come every time you call her, and sit and stay, even if you don't have food.'

I had fun testing Summer on her new skills a couple more times.

'That's enough training for one day,' said Mimi. 'Why don't you take her outside for a really good run and a play? She's been napping for most of the day so she has some excess energy she needs to burn up.'

I did as Mimi suggested, throwing a ball for Summer in the garden and trying to teach her to bring it back to me, then drop it when I said the magic words 'leave it'.

This reminded me that I still hadn't told Mum about Summer gobbling her shoe. I decided to tell her that evening over dinner. Mum would not be pleased!

After a few more minutes of rumbling and tumbling after the ball, Summer collapsed on the grass so I took her back inside the caravan. She was too little to climb the steps by herself so I had to lift her up. Summer bounded to her basket, which was tucked under the dining table, and flopped on the pillow. In one second she was fast asleep. Mission accomplished!

The caravan was filled with the delicious aroma of honey-soy chicken baking in the oven. Yay! It was one of my favourite dishes, and Mum hadn't cooked it for ages. Mum was standing at the stove, steaming greens. Harry was sitting at the table doing his homework while Bella read out loud to Mum.

In the evening we often ate dinner with Mimi and Papa on the patio. Tonight they were going out with friends, so we were having a small family meal in the caravan. I was really looking forward to enjoying some of Mum's cooking for a change. I squeezed in next to Harry and tried to doodle a picture of Summer tangled in toilet paper. It was impossible to capture how totally adorable she was.

Harry and I set the table while Mum served up dinner. Then we all sat down to eat and chat about our day.

Mum looked exhausted. Now the cafe was in business, she was leaving even earlier to open up and get ready for the first customers at seven o'clock. We were usually only just awake when Mum left, so Papa made us breakfast in their kitchen while we got ourselves up and dressed. Then Mimi and Papa walked us to school at eight-thirty.

I had felt tired after my short stint of working in the cafe yesterday. I couldn't imagine how tired Mum must be.

'So what mischief has Summer been up to now?' asked Mum with a smile.

I nearly told Mum about her shoe, guiltily hidden in the back of the cupboard, but then I didn't want to spoil her mood. And I didn't want her to think she'd made a huge mistake letting us have a puppy.

'Nothing much,' I fibbed. 'She's mostly been an angel!'

Harry snorted loudly into his orange juice.

CHAPTER 9

LOOKBOOK

It was time to get cracking on our Sassy Sisters story.

On Wednesday afternoon after school, Cici and Charlie were ready to visit some clothing shops on the main street of Kira Cove. Cici's plan was to charm, bribe or convince the store owners to let us borrow clothes for the photo shoot. She had made a folder that she called her lookbook, with a selection of photos that she had printed and pasted onto white cardboard at interesting angles. Ideas were scrawled down next to them.

Meg and I decided we would come along to offer them moral support.

The first shop we tried was a kids' boutique called Kira Beach Babes. The window was filled with child-sized mannequins wearing the latest looks.

A stylish woman stood behind the counter, folding a rainbow of singlet tops.

She looked enthusiastic when we walked in. 'Good afternoon, girls. May I help you? We have some lovely sun frocks just in from Paris.'

She waved towards a display beside the cash register. I realised there were no price tags to be seen.

'Hello,' said Cici, with her brightest smile. 'My name is Cecilia Lin and we are students from Kira Cove Primary. We're organising a fashion shoot at the beach for our school newspaper on Saturday evening and we're hoping you would lend us some clothes to photograph.'

Cici opened her lookbook to show the women what she had in mind. I took a closer look at one of the sundresses, and spotted a tag tucked in the back of the neck. I couldn't believe how expensive it was.

'I'm afraid that won't be possible,' said the woman briskly, not even glancing at the lookbook. Her welcoming smile had turned rather frosty. 'We don't lend clothes, especially not to *children* and especially not for you to wear to a *gathering* at the beach.'

'Not a gathering,' insisted Cici. 'It's a fashion shoot for our school newspaper. We can let you use some of the photos for your advertising . . .'

'Thank you all the same,' the woman interrupted Cici. 'Good day, girls.'

We were clearly dismissed. The four of us bundled out of the shop.

'Well, that didn't go so well,' said Charlie. 'I think she thought we were planning a party and wanted to steal the clothes for that.'

'On the bright side,' I said, 'we did say we wanted to focus on affordable fashion for kids. Those sundresses from Paris were two hundred dollars each!'

We strolled down the cobbled main piazza of Kira Cove, which had quaint shops and tiny restaurants on each side. A group of kids were skateboarding down a side laneway. Three boys picked up their skateboards and walked towards us.

'There's Alex, Rory and Sam,' said Meg. 'Should we ask them now if they'll be models for us?'

'Definitely,' said Charlie. She called out to them. 'Hey, guys – just wondering if you might be able to help us out?'

The boys wandered over, calling out greetings.

'We were hoping you could be models for our photo shoot on Saturday for the school newspaper?' asked Cici. She smiled at them winningly.

Alex glanced at me, his eyebrow raised in a question. 'Maybe. What would we need to wear?'

Cici flipped open her lookbook to a page that featured some of the boys' outfits she had researched.

'We haven't got the clothes yet, but here are some of the looks from the latest fashion labels,' explained Cici.

The models in the pictures wore huge sunglasses and perky fedora hats with their hands in their pockets. One wore chino shorts, a white shirt and a baby-blue linen jacket. The other had acid-yellow jeans, an electric-blue T-shirt and matching sneakers. The third model wore a shirt covered in pineapples and super-baggy hippy pants with bare feet.

'No way,' said Rory. 'I wouldn't be seen dead wearing any of that stuff!'

'Me neither,' said Alex apologetically. 'Boys we know don't want to dress like that.'

'Who did those designers make those clothes for!' said Sam. 'We'd be laughed at by the whole school if we had our photo taken looking like that.'

Cici was crushed. 'But these photos are the latest looks from the London Fashion Show.'

'Sorry, Cici,' said Alex. 'I don't reckon you'll get any of the year five boys to help you out with that one.'

The boys jumped on their skateboards and scooted off with a quick wave goodbye.

'Those boy clothes are kind of over-the-top,' I said hesitantly to Cici.

Cici tossed back her hair defiantly. 'It's *fashion.*'

'Let's try another shop,' said Meg, quickly changing the subject. 'How about that one?'

The next store was a super-cool surf shop. All the shop assistants wore singlet tops with ripped denim shorts. They were walking around, talking and laughing, and readjusting hangers on the displays. None of them seemed at all interested in helping us.

The man behind the counter had long, blond hair and a goatee beard. He didn't even try to pretend to be interested when Cici told him her spiel.

'Sorry, dudes,' he said. 'The boss won't let anyone borrow anything. Cash only, I'm afraid.'

So far, our genius idea wasn't working at all.

We were just coming out of the surf shop when we bumped into Olivia, Sienna and Willow walking along eating ice-creams.

'Hi, girls,' they chorused.

'Are you guys doing some shopping?' asked Willow. 'Doesn't look like you found anything yet.'

'No,' I said. 'We're working on our news-paper story.'

Olivia swung towards me. 'Are you inter-viewing shopkeepers?' she asked, wrinkling her nose in derision. 'That sounds boring.'

We all prickled at Olivia's words.

'No, of course not,' said Cici.

'Cici had the most brilliant idea of organising a fashion shoot,' I said quickly. 'We're just checking out ideas for different looks.'

Olivia stuck out her bottom lip. 'That sounds like an okay idea for a story,' she agreed. 'Our group has decided to interview an interesting local celebrity.'

'Who have you chosen?' asked Charlie. 'Pippa and I thought about interviewing local kids or personalities.'

'Not kids,' said Olivia, curling her lip. 'I'm going to interview Ruby Starr.'

'*Ruby Starr?*' shrieked Cici and Charlie together.

'I adore Ruby Starr,' said Charlie. Charlie could perform all the famous singer's songs on the guitar.

One of my most embarrassing experiences ever was dancing to a Ruby Starr song at school and smashing poor Alex in the face. For a while, we all thought I'd broken his nose.

'Are you really going to interview Ruby Starr?' asked Cici. 'I've heard she almost never gives interviews.'

Olivia smiled. 'Yes, I know, but my dad knows her agent and he's lined it up for me. Actually, I shouldn't tell you this, but Ruby wants to do the interview at your little cafe on Friday after school.'

'At my cafe?' I asked. 'Ruby Starr is coming to the Beach Shack?'

'Yes,' said Olivia, licking a long drip from her cookies-and-cream cone. 'I can't imagine why. She said the lemon cupcakes are to die for, but mine wasn't that great yesterday. I think it was a tad overcooked.'

I rolled my eyes at Charlie. Of course Olivia didn't like the food at my cafe. She didn't like anything about me.

'Ruby Starr said my cupcakes are to die for?' asked Cici, looking ecstatic. 'She *loves* my cupcakes!'

Technically they weren't Cici's cupcakes as my mum made them now, but I guess it was Cici's recipe so she had good reason to be excited.

'This interview is going to be fantastic,' said Sienna. 'We're so lucky that Olivia managed to organise it with Ruby. I wouldn't be surprised if our story made the front page.'

Cici didn't look quite so excited at that news. 'The front page? That would be a huge honour.'

'Anyway, we'd better go,' said Olivia, fluttering her fingers. 'We have a *looong* list of questions we need to write to ask Ruby on Friday. See you tomorrow.'

The three girls turned in a tight huddle, licking their ice-creams and discussing their burning questions for Ruby Starr.

'I really want to ask her if it's true that she's broken up with her boyfriend Kai Stone,' we overheard Olivia say as they walked off. 'I heard a rumour that's why she's here. And Sienna, I'd love it if you could take some cool photos of me with Ruby on Friday . . .'

'Great,' said Cici gloomily. 'We can't even get a shop to lend us one outfit for our photo shoot, and Olivia's group is going to get the front-page scoop with an exclusive interview with the most famous person on Kira Island.'

'I told you we should have gone with a series of fun interviews,' said Charlie. 'We could interview kids and local celebrities. I wish I'd thought of interviewing Ruby Starr.'

I felt totally disappointed. My grand visions of our Sassy Sisters club writing fun stories and taking photographs for the school newspaper were looking more and more unlikely. I scuffed a cobblestone with frustration.

'I need to get back to the boatshed,' I said

gloomily. 'I promised Mum I'd help her clean up for closing.'

'Don't worry,' said Meg. 'We'll regroup tomorrow and think of something brilliant.'

CHAPTER 10

DINO ROMPS

Meg and I walked back to the cafe together, as it was on her way home. The cafe was really quiet, so Mum said she didn't need my help after all. She and Zoe had everything under control.

'Why don't you come to my place and I can show you how to use the camera?' suggested Meg. 'It would be good if you had a chance to practise before our photo shoot.'

'Is that okay, Mum?' I asked.

'Sure, Pipkin,' said Mum. 'You can practise

using my camera later, as well. It's in the drawer under my bed.'

Meg and I went to her yacht to fetch the camera, then we sat on the jetty while Meg gave me a lesson.

'First of all, always make sure you have the strap around your neck,' said Meg. 'The camera's quite heavy and you definitely don't want to drop it!'

The camera had a long, black lens that took super-clear shots. It could be twisted to take close-up or wide-angle photos. Luckily, it had automatic functions for focusing and shutter speed, so it was quite easy to use.

'Just look through the viewfinder here,' said Meg. 'And really think about your shots. Try to get a balance of sky and ground. And use the zoom lens to get as close to the subject as you can.'

I took a whole lot of practice shots with Meg helping me, then we went for a wander up the beach, taking photos of boats bobbing, crabs rolling sand balls, pelicans fishing, and kids cycling past. Meg was really encouraging and gave me tips on how to make the photos better. We took loads of shots and then deleted all the duds, which was most of them!

Later, back at home, I borrowed Mum's camera and took dozens of photos of adorable Summer — pouncing on a blade of grass, chasing a butterfly, running off with Bella's toy dinosaur, collapsing asleep in her basket curled up with her favourite toy. I also snapped some shots of Papa cooking in the kitchen, and Mimi feeding the chickens.

Harry was wearing the black top hat and magician's cape that my dad had bought him back in London. He was practising magic tricks on the patio by the outdoor table.

Magic was one of the things that Dad and Harry had loved doing together. Dad had taught Harry some really cool card tricks and had taken him to see some of the greatest magicians of modern times. Lately, Harry had been practising his tricks more than ever. Perhaps it made him feel closer to Dad.

Today he was working with a clear plastic bottle filled with water and several sachets of tomato sauce that he'd borrowed from the cafe.

'Hello, Master Magician,' I said. 'What scintillating enchantments are you creating now?'

'Look, Pippa,' said Harry, popping a sachet of sauce inside the full bottle and screwing the lid on tight. 'With just the power of my mind I can make the tomato sauce sink.'

Harry concentrated hard, holding the bottle with one hand. 'Down,' he commanded in a deep, confident voice, lowering his other hand in a downward signal. Obediently the sachet dropped to the bottom of the bottle.

'Up,' he commanded, raising his hand again. The sachet of tomato sauce bobbed to the top of the bottle. 'Down again. Now stop!' The sachet hovered in the middle of the bottle of water.

'That's incredible, Harry,' I said, snapping some close-ups of his face, which was furrowed with concentration. 'You're getting really good at this.'

Harry beamed at me and the sachet bobbed to the top again. 'Thanks, Pippa,' he replied. 'I need to be perfect if I'm going to be a professional magician one day.'

Looking for my next model, Bella agreed to pose so I could practise taking fashion shots, but she insisted on wearing her dinosaur tail. That worked well until Summer discovered the enticingly waving green tail and attacked. She pounced and wrestled, snapping and growling.

I captured a series of close-ups of tubby Summer tumbling over the green tail.

'*Muuum*,' roared Bella, stomping her foot. 'Summer's eating my tail and Pippa's not helping.'

'Grrrr,' replied Summer.

I quickly stopped taking photographs, set the camera on the patio table and put on my firmest voice. 'Leave it, Summer.'

Summer shook her head from side to side ferociously, her needle-sharp teeth buried in the poor dino tail. I tried to prise her jaws apart but ended up with a sharp nip to the palm of my hand.

'Ouch,' I yelled. 'That hurt! Naughty Summer.' I sucked the blood from the scratches.

Summer looked sorry for just a moment, putting her head down on her paws and gazing up at me with her big brown eyes. But then Bella's dino tail waggled again and Summer was off.

Mum came running out from the caravan. 'Is everything all right, Bella-boo?'

'*Noooo*,' shouted Bella, grabbing her tail with both hands. 'Let go, you wicked puppy.'

Bella was now shaking her tail from side to side, trying to dislodge Summer. Summer, of course, thought it was all part of the wonderful game and hung on even tighter. I tried to pull Summer off but she was as slippery as a greased piglet.

Mum laughed out loud to see our struggle.

'It's not funny,' bellowed Bella. 'She's destroying my tail!'

'Summer, leave it,' said Mum in her sternest voice. At once, Summer dropped the fluffy appendage and looked up at Mum for approval, pink tongue lolling and plumed tail wagging madly. 'Summer, come.'

Summer raced to Mum's foot and sat on it. 'Good girl. That's a perfect puppy dog.' Mum scooped Summer up for a cuddle, kissing her on the nose. Summer wriggled her whole body in ecstasy.

'Come on, Pipkin,' said Mum. 'Let's go and wash that puppy bite. And Bella-boo, maybe your dinosaur tail should go away in the cupboard for a while.'

The next morning at school, Charlie and Cici reported that they'd tried three more shops yesterday afternoon but with no luck at all. At recess, we asked Jack and Seb if they'd model for us, but they took one look at Cici's lookbook and flatly refused.

Thursday lunchtime was the second meeting of the Kira Cove School Newspaper Club. It was a little worrying because quite a few kids seemed to have dropped out. Perhaps their story ideas had become too difficult, just like ours.

We all sat around on beanbags in the library. Mrs Neill started the meeting by asking everyone how their stories were going.

Olivia, Sienna, Willow and Tash looked very pleased with themselves.

'We've organised an interview with Ruby Starr on Friday afternoon,' Olivia announced proudly.

A murmur of excitement ran through the whole group.

'Ruby Starr is one of the most popular singers with kids our age,' said Willow. 'She's an absolute sensation.'

'I know who Ruby Starr is,' said Mrs Neill, suppressing a smile. 'Well, congratulations, girls. That is an incredible scoop.'

Olivia nodded seriously. 'I know, Mrs Neill. Ruby never gives interviews normally, but she made a special exception for us. I probably shouldn't tell you, but we'll be meeting her at the Beach Shack to have afternoon tea, take some photographs and ask her a long list of questions about her life and career.'

'Ruby Starr will be at the Beach Shack on Friday afternoon?' asked Seb. 'That story plus a huge photograph will be fantastic for our front cover.'

The other year six kids nodded.

Jack examined his list of stories. 'If you get a good interview we can continue the story

95

with more pictures on page three. Then I've reserved pages six and seven for the fashion shoot story, followed by the back three pages for our sport stories.'

Olivia shot me a look of triumph. I slumped down in my beanbag.

Great! I thought. *Olivia and her team get the front page and our feature is tucked up the back before sport!*

Seb looked serious. 'So if anyone has any bright ideas, we still need to fill three or four news pages.'

No one seemed to have any suggestions, or perhaps it was that no one wanted to take on more work.

Mrs Neill turned towards us. 'And how are you girls going?'

Charlie, Cici, Meg and I all looked at each other. We didn't want to admit to Mrs Neill that we hadn't made much progress.

'Well,' said Charlie. 'We hope to do the shoot on Saturday afternoon and we're just organising all the details.'

'Like the clothes and models and accessories,' said Cici.

Mrs Neill nodded. 'I like the idea of a fashion shoot but perhaps you could make it more meaningful than just photographs of clothes. Is there some way you could make the concept stronger? You do have two whole pages to fill.'

'Great,' I whispered to Charlie. 'We were having trouble organising the clothes and the models as it was. Now we have to make the concept stronger as well.'

'Maybe it's all too hard,' complained Charlie. 'Maybe we should just give the whole thing a miss.'

Seb glared at his stepsister. 'Don't be silly, Charlie. We need ten pages of stories by next week! We need all the material we can get.'

CHAPTER 11

FRIDAY FRENZY

On Friday there was a definite buzz around the school. At recess, Bella came running up to me in huge excitement.

'Pippa! Did you know that Ruby Starr is coming to our cafe this afternoon?' she demanded. 'All my friends want to come along to meet her.'

I felt my heart sink. 'How did you hear about it, Bella?'

'My friend Daisy told me – you know,

Charlie's little sister?' announced Bella. 'I can't believe you didn't tell me. You know how much I love her music.'

'I didn't know you even knew who Ruby Starr was!' I retorted. 'You certainly hadn't heard of her a few weeks ago.'

Bella shook her head in disgust. '*Everyone* knows Ruby Starr.'

It seemed everyone did. On Friday afternoons we always did school sport at the beach. Our group did kayaking. I hadn't been doing it for very long but I felt like I was finally improving. I really looked forward to our afternoon splashing out on the water. We had races, accidentally-on-purpose capsized into the water, gossiped and looked out for the pod of super-friendly Kira Cove dolphins. But there was no sign of them today.

The four of us paddled out into the middle of the cove. Charlie and I were in one kayak, and Cici and Meg were in another. When we were far enough from the shore, we pulled our paddles in and floated, enjoying the lapping of the water against the sides of the kayaks and the screeching of the seagulls. A pelican sailed through the sky then landed with a loud plop close by.

'Well, it's Friday afternoon, and we need to do this photo shoot tomorrow,' said Cici. 'And we're still no closer to finding some clothes to feature.'

'We could visit some more shops after school today, instead of having our meeting,' suggested Meg, although she didn't sound very keen. Meg wasn't much of a shopper. Usually, the four of us met every Friday afternoon after school for our Sassy Sisters meeting. We took it in turns to meet at one another's houses or at the Beach Shack, have afternoon tea and hang out. It was always so much fun. But this week I couldn't.

'I'm sorry but I can't come today,' I said.

'I promised Mum I'd help at the cafe after school. Apparently she has a heap of bookings.'

'That's okay. Cici and I can go by ourselves,' said Charlie. 'I know you'd rather not come, Meg. And maybe the shops will be more willing if there are fewer of us. There are still a couple of shops in the back streets that we haven't tried yet.'

'I hope we can find someone to lend us clothes,' wailed Cici. 'We're cutting it *sooo* fine.'

'What about asking your mum if we can feature some of her clothes?' suggested Charlie.

Cici shook her head. 'I could borrow some things but I didn't want it to be a Nathalie Lin Design feature. Besides, the boys are right. We want it to be everyday clothes that kids would love to wear. Not just high fashion that's expensive and impractical.'

I thought about Cici's sense of style. She had the most fantastic wardrobe I'd ever seen. Charlie also had some beautiful boho-hippy dresses. I'd love to own some of their clothes.

I sat up suddenly. 'You want it to be everyday clothes that kids would want to wear, right?'

'Sure,' said Cici and Charlie together.

'Well, instead of borrowing new clothes, why don't we just raid your wardrobe?' I asked Cici. 'Charlie has some cool stuff too. And we could ask the boys to model for us, but just wear some of their favourite clothes and you can style them.'

'That's a brilliant idea,' said Meg. 'Cici has all the accessories too – bags, belts, shoes, jewellery . . .'

Cici and Charlie looked at each other, then at me.

'Yes!' said Charlie.

I could see Cici's mind ticking over as she thought about the outfits she could pull together.

'If you guys come over to my place tomorrow morning, we can go through some clothes and decide what to shoot,' said Cici. 'Then we'll meet up again at about three o'clock at the Beach Shack to get everyone dressed, ready to start taking photos on the beach around four.'

We paddled in to shore, feeling exhilarated that we had a new plan. We dragged the kayaks back up the beach, hosed them off and put them away in the shed.

After sport, the kids usually hung around, chatting and joking. But not today. Everyone seemed keen to get away.

I went back to school to pick up Bella and Harry. The younger kids like Bella didn't go outside the school for sport, and Harry had chosen to play touch football in the grounds rather than doing a water sport. He was still playing with a group of friends and Bella was swinging on the monkey bars.

As usual it took ages to extract my little sister. Finally I had to threaten to tell Mum that she'd been naughty.

'You don't have to be so huffy,' said Bella, climbing down from the bars.

'Huffy!' I cried. 'I've been asking you to come down for ten minutes!'

Harry came running as soon as he saw Bella's feet touch the ground. He wasn't going to waste time standing around waiting for her. Even so, it was later than usual when we finally reached the Beach Shack.

I could tell something was different walking down the drive. There was a hubbub of noise and a queue of people waiting outside. Inside, the cafe was jam-packed.

Every table was taken and people were standing at the long bench and in huddles in every spare corner. Mum and Zoe looked completely frazzled. Zoe was pumping out drinks, while Mum was trying to keep up with the orders being shouted across the bar.

'I'll have six lemon cupcakes, please,' yelled a woman in front of us, who was standing with her two daughters.

'So sorry, ma'am,' said Mum, raising her voice over the din. 'But we've completely sold out of cupcakes. I do have a couple of date slices left, or some choc-chunk cookies?'

The woman huffed with annoyance. 'I'll take the slice.'

One of the daughters, a year six girl from school, pouted. 'I don't want the slice. Ruby Starr loves the *cupcakes*.'

The other daughter, from year three, craned her head towards the entrance. 'She should be here any minute.'

I noticed that Olivia, Sienna, Tash and Willow were seated at the round table in the corner – my favourite table – with a three-tiered stand in front of them piled high with lemon cupcakes. They sipped nervously on chocolate milkshakes as they waited for the pop singer to arrive.

Mum caught sight of us through the crowd and waved frantically at me. 'Can you come and help us?' she mouthed.

So for the next half an hour Harry and I ran back and forth, delivering drinks and plates of food, clearing tables, washing glasses and cups, and generally helping in any way we could. Almost every kid from our school seemed to be here.

Mrs Beecham was sitting at her usual table with a friend. She waved me over imperiously.

'What on earth's going on, Philippa?' Mrs Beecham demanded in an extremely crotchety tone. 'What are all these rambunctious children doing here? And why hasn't Zoe brought our Prince of Wales tea? Mrs Fowles and I were looking forward to a *quiet* cup of tea and a chat. But we can't hear ourselves think!'

'I'm so sorry, Mrs Beecham,' I said. She must be upset if she was calling me Philippa. She hadn't called me that for weeks. 'All the kids from school are here because they think a pop star's coming in today.'

'A *pop* star?' asked Mrs B. 'How utterly dreadful.'

'I'll go and get your tea right now,' I said soothingly. 'Zoe's a little rushed off her feet.'

I raced to the kitchen and made Mrs Beecham's tea, using a pretty floral teapot with matching cups and jug. Luckily, I know exactly how she likes it. I popped two choc-chunk cookies on a plate and carried them back to her table.

'Thank you, Pippa,' said Mrs Beecham, looking relieved. 'I knew I could count on you.'

As I was carrying away a tray of dirty dishes, I noticed an older girl come just inside the front door. She was wearing torn jeans, cowboy boots, a loose white T-shirt and big dark sunglasses. She had long golden-brown hair and a black floppy hat on her head.

The girl took one look at the chaos of the crowded Beach Shack, spun on her heels and left. I didn't blame her.

Still, Olivia and her gang waited in their corner, anxiously nibbling on cupcakes. Olivia had a piece of paper she kept reading over. Willow had her phone set up ready to record. Tash jiggled up and down, while Sienna kept scanning the crowds looking for a familiar face.

'I don't think she's coming,' I overheard the year six girl say to her Mum.

'She probably wasn't ever coming,' her mother said. 'It must have been a publicity stunt by the cafe. It certainly worked – the place is overflowing. '

After an hour, people started to leave in dribs and drabs. At last there was just Olivia, Sienna, Willow and Tash, waiting there in the corner.

Zoe began cleaning the coffee machine. Mum started to tally up the receipts and cash. The good news was that there was piles of it!

Harry and I kept clearing debris from the surrounding tables and rinsing the crockery. Bella's job was to fluff all the cushions and collect all the dirty napkins. We packed the dishwasher together, ready to switch it on.

Mum went over to the round table where the girls were sitting. 'I'm sorry, girls, but it's five o'clock so it's time for you to go home. We're closing up now.'

'But we're waiting for someone really important to arrive,' pleaded Olivia. 'She's running late but she'll be here any moment.'

'I don't think she'll come now,' said Mum kindly. 'Maybe she was put off by the number of people here today. I wouldn't blame her.'

Olivia's eyes filled with tears. She blinked rapidly, then tossed her high, dark ponytail.

'Come on, girls,' she said. 'Let's go.'

Olivia marched past without looking at me, followed by the others. Willow and Sienna gave me a weak smile as they left. I helped Mum clear the last table.

'So who was the big celebrity everyone was so keen to meet at our humble little cafe?' asked Mum.

'A famous pop singer called Ruby Starr,' I said. 'I don't think anyone was meant to know she was coming but Olivia told a few people, just to show off, then the whole school found out.'

Mum nodded. 'I thought it must be something like that. I think poor Olivia learned a very hard lesson today.'

I had to agree. And, surprisingly, I felt really sorry for her.

CHAPTER 12

CICI'S BOUDOIR

The Sassy Sisters had arranged to meet at Cici's house at ten o'clock on Saturday morning. Charlie and Meg rode their bikes. I walked the five minutes from Mimi's house.

Cici lived in one of the quiet back streets of Kira Cove, in a small white cottage built on the side of the hill. In the front garden there was a paved terrace with star jasmine growing over the trellis, and terracotta pots of flaming-pink geraniums. A pair of French doors led into the front room. We walked through the open doors into a bright and sunny studio that was filled with vibrant colours and objects. One wall was covered with a giant black fabric board, with fashion photographs, swatches of material, postcards of butterflies and peacocks and pencil sketches pinned up. This was Nathalie's mood board that Cici had reminded me about.

Two headless mannequins stood in a corner, wearing evening dresses of shimmering silk and lace. In the middle of the room was a huge antique table, which was spread with rolls of material, piles of papers and thick, black folios. An ornate sign hung over the door saying, 'Nathalie Lin Design'.

Cici's puggle, Muffin, came running up to give each of us a welcome lick. Charlie scooped her up in her arms for a cuddle.

'Mum has a big deadline so she's working all weekend,' explained Cici. 'She just got back from visiting the fashion shows in Italy.'

'It must be nice to have her home again,' I replied.

'Yes,' said Cici, with a huge grin. 'Especially because she always brings me back presents. This time she bought me some gorgeous sandals and the cutest sundress.'

Cici's mum was on the phone, but she waved to us as we came in. We heard snatches of her conversation about spring stories, runway shows and delivery dates.

We crept through the studio and into a hallway that led past a number of bedrooms until we came to a huge open-plan kitchen and family room out the back. The windows looked out onto the tropical garden on the steep hillside. As always, Cici's kitchen smelled of melted butter and sweet treats.

Cici's dad, Eric, was sitting at the kitchen table reading a newspaper.

'Hello, girls,' he said. 'I hear you have a big day planned?'

We all said hi in return and chatted to him about our ideas.

'Dad and I got up early this morning to bake something for the shoot,' said Cici. With a flourish she showed us a multi-tiered cake stand piled high with delicate lemony iced cupcakes.

'Yummo,' I said. 'The boys will definitely help us with that kind of bribery.'

Eric was a pastry chef for the grandest hotel on Kira Island. At work he created terribly complicated desserts that were like works of art. But at home, he made the best little cakes and yummy treats, so we loved coming to Cici's house. Eric had been a massive help for my mum, giving her advice and recipes for the cafe menu (and saving us from seaweed gloop and sawdust!).

'A promise of cake was the only way I could get Alex and Rory to come along,' confessed Cici. 'So we made a double batch.'

'Great thinking,' said Meg.

'So let's get to work,' said Charlie. 'Where are those clothes?'

'Come into my *boudoir*,' said Cici, mimicking a strong French accent.

Cici's bedroom, like everything about her, was quirky, stylish and very neat. Picture windows draped with filmy white chiffon overlooked the sunny garden. Music was playing – a song by Ruby Starr.

In one corner, the bed was covered in a mossy-green quilt with large appliquéd polka-dots of turquoise, hot-pink, orange and yellow, with matching piles of pillows and cushions. A white replica reindeer head was hung on the walls, with an orange scarf wrapped around its neck and hot-pink baubles dangling from its antlers. A fluffy brown teddy bear sat in the middle of all the cushions.

A heart-shaped mood-board hung over Cici's desk with photographs of Muffin, family portraits and snapshots of friends. I was thrilled to see a photograph of the four of us with our arms around each other, all dressed up and ready for the grand opening party for the Beach Shack.

'I love that photo,' said Charlie. 'Wasn't that a fun day?'

'The best,' I said.

The far wall was a long bank of built-in wardrobes. Cici flung open the door to reveal shelves of neatly folded clothes, dresses on hangers, racks of boots and shoes and rows of drawers.

'This is what I was thinking,' said Cici, pulling out armfuls of clothes and piling them on the bed. Cici showed us different combinations of shorts and T-shirts, sundresses, jeans and tops, party dresses and beachwear. 'I thought Meg could wear this cute playsuit, while this would look adorable on Pippa.'

Cici handed me an aqua polka-dot sundress and a pair of bejewelled leather sandals. The sandal straps were decorated with chunky tur-quoise stones and dazzling diamantes. I slipped them on.

'These sandals are so pretty,' I said, spinning around so the jewels sparkled.

'Mum just brought them back from Italy,' explained Cici. 'They're going to be the hottest trend next summer.'

Cici had loads of clothes, so of course we had to try everything on. Then we experimented with different summery accessories and jewel-lery. While we started out being sensible, we were soon giggling, mismatching clothes and going completely, kookily over the top.

Meg found a pair of cat ears to wear, with black stockings as a tail, odd-coloured socks and black whiskers drawn on her face. Charlie wore stripy socks on her hands as mittens, a feather boa with a diamante tiara and bumble-bee tights. Cici wore the loudest clothes she could find in garish orange, lime-green and turquoise, all layered over the top of each other.

My look was punk meets fairy: a hot-pink tulle tutu, black leather jacket, black leggings, fingerless gloves, chunky lace-up boots and a silver lamé scarf tied around my head.

Cici sucked in her cheeks like a supermodel, pursed her lips and opened her eyes wide. 'Don't we look *adorable*, darlings!'

We pouted, preened and posed. We took selfies with our tongues poked out, eyes crossed and crazy hand gestures. I laughed until my cheeks ached.

After we had gone through all the outfits, we helped Cici to pack them up into two overnight bags. Then she gave us each an outfit to get changed into ready for the shoot. Mine was the sparkly jewelled sandals, white jeans and a swirly indigo-and-white camisole top.

'All set,' said Meg, twitching her little cat nose.

'Not quite,' said Cici, fetching a fistful of

bottles from her dressing table. 'It wouldn't be a Sassy Sisters fashion party without nail polish. Take your pick – periwinkle blue, orange, pastel pink, silver, amethyst or sapphire?'

'I'll have periwinkle blue,' I said, taking the bottle from Cici's outstretched hand. I loved to paint my nails the colour of the Kira sky.

CHAPTER 13

SATURATED

As planned, the four of us walked to the cafe at three o'clock. We were all dressed and accessorised, ready for the photo shoot.

Cici looked super-stylish in an orange skirt, white singlet top, denim jacket and brown ankle boots. Charlie was very boho-chic in a floating, floral dress with strappy leather sandals. Most of her golden hair was flowing loose, except for a thick braid framing the left side of her face. Meg was looking sporty and natural in denim shorts, a grey T-shirt, canvas sneakers and her bobbed hair pulled back in a short ponytail. We all looked gorgeous in our different ways.

But something dreadful had happened. The Kira sky, normally a deep periwinkle blue, had turned dark. Thundery grey clouds rolled in from the horizon. The air felt restless and heavy.

'It looks like it's going to rain,' wailed Charlie, peering up at the ominous sky.

'But it never rains on Kira Island,' I said with disbelief. In fact, when I first moved here and was feeling totally miserable, I missed the drizzly London streets. Now I loved the vast blues of the Kira sea and sky.

The heavens answered with a clap of thunder, then torrents of rain poured from above. We sheltered in the front door of the cafe, barely able to see a few metres in front of us.

'When it does rain here, it really pours!' said Cici. 'It's like a waterfall out there.'

'We can't take photos in this weather,' said Meg.

'Why don't we take all our things upstairs to my room?' I suggested. 'And maybe it will clear up in a little while.'

We gathered the tote bags and lugged them upstairs. On the way to my room I gave my friends a quick tour to see how the builders were coming along. The kitchen cupboards were finished now, but there was no benchtop or appliances yet. The view through the floor-to-ceiling windows was of thick, dreary grey clouds and torrential rain. It was almost impossible to tell where the sky ended and the sea began.

We took the bags into my room.

'What's this?' asked Cici, gazing at the left-hand wall.

There was one change in my room that I was rather proud of.

'It's my mood board,' I replied. 'I took your advice and it really helped to inspire me.'

I had stuck up loads of photos from Mum's interior design magazines, as well as images from the internet to form a collage of ideas and colours. I'd also stuck up some of my sketches of seahorses, starfish and frangipani flowers, along with some of the paint colour chips that Mum had brought home.

In London, we had lived in an old Victorian terrace, with high ceilings and ornate plasterwork. My bedroom had a fireplace with a white-painted mantelpiece, plush grey carpet and French doors opening onto a tiny wrought-iron balcony. It had been painted a soft dove-grey, with pops of rose-pink in the cushions, rugs and accessories.

Thinking of my old room gave me that hollow feeling of missing London all over again. Missing my friends, my school, but most of all my dad. So, when planning my new Kira

Island bedroom, I wanted it to be completely different. The girls crowded around, examining the pictures on the wall.

'I love that one,' said Charlie, pointing to a photo of a blue room with a big white bed and a filmy canopy hanging above it.

'How cute is that little window seat?' said Meg, looking at another cut-out.

'I want a really beachy, tropical theme for my new room, a bit like this one.' I pointed to a big photo that I'd printed off the internet. 'I'm thinking white walls and white furniture, with splashes of turquoise and sea-green for the cushions and rugs. And I'm going to have fun accessories like seashells, frangipanis and starfish scattered around.'

Cici nodded with approval. 'That sounds adorable. Where are you going to put everything?'

I looked around. The room was empty

except for the cupboard built on the right side of my window.

'The bed over there.' I waved towards the left wall. 'Floor-to-ceiling bookshelves on the other side of the window. A sunny window seat in the middle, with lots of cushions. It will be a perfect place to read and draw.'

Cici's idea of the mood-board had helped me to visualise it all so clearly.

'When do you think it will be finished?' asked Charlie.

'Mum says just another few weeks,' I said. 'I can't wait!'

Just then, Mum's voice sounded faintly from downstairs, calling to us.

'It must be the boys here for the photo shoot,' said Meg. We clattered down the stairs. Alex and Rory were waiting just inside the open front door. It was still pouring outside.

The boys had arrived dressed in their favourite clothes – brightly coloured board shorts, loose T-shirts and canvas sneakers. They were both completely drenched and Rory carried a football.

'Hi, girls,' said Alex, wringing out the hem of his T-shirt. 'Are we going to get started?'

'No,' said Cici, grumpily. 'The weather's too awful.'

'Don't let a bit of water stop us,' said Rory, tossing his ball up in the air. 'One of our favourite things to do is play footy in the rain!'

Cici rolled her eyes. 'Nice try.'

'It is meant to be photos of things kids love,' I reminded everyone.

'We can reschedule the photo shoot for tomorrow afternoon,' said Meg.

Alex shook his head. 'Sorry. I've got a family barbeque tomorrow afternoon.'

'And I promised to help my mum with some chores at home,' added Rory, throwing the football to Alex.

'So it's now or never,' I said. 'Come on,

let's take photos of the boys playing footy in the rain.'

We borrowed two umbrellas from the Beach Shack and ventured outside. I didn't want to ruin Cici's new sandals so I stowed them in my backpack in the cafe and went barefoot instead.

Cici directed from under one umbrella, with Charlie huddled beside her. Her grumpiness soon evaporated.

I held another umbrella for Meg, while she took the photos using her mum's camera. I was itching to take some photos myself. The boys ran up and down the beach, kicking the ball to each other. It actually looked really fun. Soon Meg couldn't resist.

'Are you okay taking these shots for a few minutes, Pippa?' she asked.

'Sure,' I said. Meg handed me her camera and quickly reminded me how to use it. Then she kicked off her shoes and ran towards the boys.

'Over here, Alex,' she called. Alex obliged and threw her the ball. Meg took aim and kicked it up the beach. Rory gave chase so Meg raced off after him.

When Meg joined the game, Charlie slipped her sandals off and ran after the others too.

It was tricky taking photos in the pouring rain. We had to juggle the umbrellas and our models insisted on tearing up and down the beach after the ball.

'Cici, can I come under your umbrella?' I asked. 'I can't shoot and balance mine at the same time.'

So Cici walked us up and down, sheltering the camera while I shot photo after photo. Charlie and Meg were soon drenched too, but laughed as they kicked up sand and vied for the ball. Charlie kicked the ball to Rory, who trapped it and sprinted off up the beach. Alex and Meg gave chase. Rory kicked the ball away but Meg intercepted it and raced back down the beach to score a goal.

Meg jumped up and did a victory dance in the rain. I snapped a close-up of her beaming face.

After a few more minutes, we all headed back inside the empty cafe, where I showed the photos I'd taken to Cici and the others. It was my first attempt at sports photography so I wasn't surprised that the first few shots had missing heads or partial bodies or were just a blur of movement. But the later ones were definitely an improvement.

'I love that one,' said Cici, pointing at a shot of Meg's sand-smudged face.

'You took some fantastic photos, Pippa,' said Meg. 'They're really fun and natural.'

'Well, Cici did say she didn't want boring department store catalogue shots,' I joked.

'They show our theme perfectly: what kids love to do,' Charlie added. 'Run in the rain, play footy, dance . . .'

'This is a fantastic start,' said Cici. 'I can't wait to take some more tomorrow when the sun's out!'

CHAPTER 14

DOGGY DISASTER

On Sunday morning I woke up early but it was still pouring with rain. The four of us checked in with each other later in the day, but there was nothing for it but to postpone the photo shoot again.

It was so frustrating. There were only four days left until the newspaper had to be finished. Time was running out.

It was squishy enough living in a caravan on a normal day, but when it was pouring with rain everyone got cabin fever. Mum had gone to the shops to buy food for the week, Mimi and Papa were in the cottage and Harry was on his bunk reading a book about the life of Harry Houdini, a famous escape artist and magician.

I dragged out my backpack, which I'd taken to the photo shoot yesterday, and rummaged through it, looking for my notebook and pencils.

I dropped the backpack next to my bunk and sat cross-legged on the floor, doodling pictures of Summer, who was curled up in her basket fast asleep. She looked totally adorable and angelic, although I didn't know how she could sleep.

Bella was on Mum's bed playing with her dinosaur collection. The stegosaurus was eating the herd of iguanodons, which involved lots of roaring and stomping and gnashing.

Thankfully, Mimi popped her head around the door. 'I thought you all might like to come inside and watch a movie? It's too wet to do much else.'

Harry slammed his book shut. 'Can we watch an action movie?'

'Sure,' said Mimi. 'Just as long as it's not too scary.'

'What about that one about the escaping dinosaurs?' suggested Bella. 'Where everyone gets eaten?'

Bella roared and leapt off the bed, scattering plastic toys everywhere.

'No way,' I replied, jumping to my feet and dropping my notebook on the table. 'How about the one with the academy for kid spies?'

'I've seen that one,' said Harry. 'But there's a really good comedy about a school football team that loses every game. You'd love it.'

We followed Mimi back to the house, dodging puddles as we argued over the best movie to watch. Papa made popcorn for us. We all sat in the dark, watching the football movie on the big TV screen.

After about half an hour, there was a funny scene where the hero's dog ran onto the field in the middle of the game and ruined everything.

'*Summer,*' I said suddenly. I'd forgotten all about her, fast asleep in her basket. Papa paused the movie.

'Mimi, can I just check on Summer?' I asked. 'She's probably still asleep but I should go and look.'

'Good idea, Pippa,' said Mimi. 'Why don't you bring her over here so we can keep an eye on her?'

I dashed across the garden through the rain to the caravan. I flung open the door and leapt up the stairs.

As I stepped inside, my heart sunk into my boots. Summer was awake. She bounded toward me, her pink tongue lolling out and a trail of destruction in her wake.

Dinosaurs had been beheaded, paper was torn into tiny scraps and my backpack was gaping open, its contents spread across the floor. Scattered through the mess were tiny glittery beads.

'Summer!' I shouted in horror. I leaned down and picked up one of the beads. It was a turquoise gemstone. It looked horribly, terrifyingly familiar. Where had Summer found a turquoise gem?

I stooped down and checked under the table in Summer's bed. There, snuggled among the cushions, was a flat, leather sandal. Feeling sick, I pulled it out.

It was, of course, Cici's brand-new sandal – a present from her mother, all the way from Italy. And now it was covered in hundreds of tiny tooth marks. Summer had ripped every diamante and gemstone off the straps and strewn them over the floor.

But that was not all. Finally, she had gnawed a large gouge out of the heel. The sandal was completely ruined. What was I going to say to Cici? How could I ever fix this?

'Summer, you naughty, naughty dog,' I cried. 'This is all your fault.'

Tears welled up. I sank down onto the floor, holding the sandal in disbelief. Summer bounded up to me and licked me all over the face. She gave me an adorable puppy grin. I pushed her away, feeling furious and ill.

Maybe I could hide the sandal and pretend nothing had happened. But Cici would want to see the shoes at the photo shoot tomorrow. Maybe Mum would ring Cici's mum and apologise?

Summer looked up at me, her head cocked to one side. She didn't understand why I'd pushed her away. She whined and pawed at my leg.

I picked Summer up and cuddled her close. I had to remember that she was just a puppy.

As Mimi said, it was up to me to use my human brain to make sure she couldn't get into trouble. It wasn't really Summer's fault. I shouldn't have left my backpack on the floor where she could reach it. I shouldn't have left her all alone in the caravan with so much temptation. It was all my fault.

What could I do? Mum always reminded me to have courage. But what would Mum advise me to do now?

The first thing to do was to clean up this mess so that Summer couldn't swallow any of the wreckage. I popped Summer in her basket and crawled around picking up diamantes and dinosaur heads. All Bella's dinosaur toys went in a container on the kitchen counter. Cici's sandals, plus all the gemstones I could find, went in a plastic bag inside my backpack. Luckily I found lots, which probably meant Summer hadn't swallowed any.

I fished around in my bottom drawer

until I found my wallet. There was thirty dollars in there. My life savings from helping Mum in the cafe and the last of my birthday money. The money I was saving to buy a new swimming costume so Olivia couldn't sneer at me anymore. The swimming costume I so badly wanted so I could fit in with the other girls.

The safest place for Summer was with Mimi and Papa in the cottage. Mimi checked that Summer was all right and promised to keep a close eye on her. A very close eye!

Armed with a raincoat and my backpack, I set off to Cici's house. The rain poured down, soaking my hair and seeping down the back of my neck. As I came closer my feet dragged. I had to force myself to keep walking until I finally reached Cici's front door.

I knocked and the door opened. It was Cici's mum, Nathalie.

'Hello, Pippa,' she said. 'Have you come to see Cici?'

'Hi, Nathalie,' I said. Did my voice have a telltale wobble? 'Yes. Is she home?'

'Of course. Come in out of the rain. Cici's just been telling me all about your fashion shoot for the school newspaper. What a shame it's been washed out.'

I took off my dripping raincoat and stepped into Nathalie's crowded, colourful studio. As always, the house smelled of something yummy baking in the oven.

Just then Cici and Muffin popped around the corner. 'Pippa?' called Cici. 'I thought I heard your voice.'

I stood near the doorway, feeling frightened and small. Perhaps I should go home and get Mum to explain everything instead? I wished Nathalie wasn't there so I could just tell Cici.

'Pippa?' repeated Cici. 'Do you want to come in and taste my new invention?'

Have courage, I told myself. Just get it over with. I took a very deep breath.

'Cici, Nathalie,' I began. 'I'm so terribly sorry. But something dreadful has happened.'

'Is everything all right?' asked Nathalie, looking concerned.

'Are you okay?' asked Cici. 'Is someone hurt?'

'Not exactly,' I said. 'It's Summer . . .'

I opened my backpack and pulled out the pair of sandals – one perfect and one destroyed.

Cici gasped in shock. The look on her face made me gabble before my courage fled.

'I left my backpack on the floor and Summer discovered your beautiful new sandals . . . I'm so very sorry. I've brought all my pocket money so I can buy you some new ones. I know it's not enough but I can earn some more working for Mum at the cafe. Just tell me how much they cost and I'll pay you every cent, I promise.'

I took a breath. Cici took the ruined sandal from my hand and turned it over and over. Her face was shocked and disgusted. Cici must hate me. She'd never forgive me. Oh, why had I left my backpack on the floor where Summer could find it?

I felt the tears welling up again and blinked them away. I pulled my wallet from my backpack and shoved the thirty dollars into Cici's hands. Cici still didn't say anything, she simply stared at the chewed sandal.

'Is Summer all right?' asked Nathalie. 'She didn't make herself sick swallowing anything?'

'No,' I replied. 'Mimi checked her and she seems fine.'

'Thank goodness,' said Nathalie. 'That's the most important thing.'

'How could you let Summer get them?' Cici asked, pushing the money back at me. 'I'd never have let you borrow my best shoes if I thought you'd be so careless.'

'I'm so sorry, Cici. I didn't mean to . . .' My voice trailed off. There was nothing else I could say.

Nathalie put her hand on Cici's shoulder, then gave me a hug. 'It's okay, Pippa. Thank you for coming around to tell us. It was brave of you. And thanks for offering to pay to replace them.'

'We can't replace them,' snapped Cici. 'You bought them in Italy. It was my present.'

Nathalie looked at Cici sternly.

'I know you're upset, Cici,' said Nathalie. 'But we *can* replace them. I can phone my supplier in Italy and he can post us another pair. They can be here within a week.'

'Really?' I asked hopefully. 'Are they very expensive? It might take me a while to save up but I promise I'll pay you the money.'

'Thanks, Pippa, but this money will be

enough,' Nathalie assured me. 'And I don't want you to worry about it anymore. It's just a pair of shoes and Cici has plenty. No one was hurt. Summer is fine, so everything is easily fixed.'

Cici looked shamefaced. 'I'm sorry too, Pippa. Of course it doesn't matter.' She grinned at me. 'And it's good to know that Summer has fantastic taste! Do you remember, Mum, when Muffin was a puppy and ate your brand-new designer heels?'

'How could I forget?' said Nathalie. 'Those shoes cost a fortune!'

I felt giddy with relief. Cici wasn't mad with me anymore. Which reminded me that I really needed to confess to Mum that Summer had eaten her shoes too. I made up my mind to do it that night over dinner. Or maybe at bedtime?

CHAPTER 15

PUPPY TALK

On the walk home I decided that something needed to be done about Summer and her wicked ways. Luckily, I bumped into the perfect person. Charlie overtook me as she rode her bike along the beachfront. Her two border collies, Zorro and Bandit, were running beside her. The rain had slowed to a misty drizzle.

'Hey, Pippa. I was just coming to see you,' said Charlie. She jumped off her bike and wheeled it along beside me. Zorro and

Bandit wagged their tails so hard that their whole bodies wiggled from side to side.

'Hi, Charlie. Hi, Zorro and Bandit,' I gave both dogs a good rub behind the ears. They looked up at me adoringly. They were the most beautiful dogs, with their shaggy black-and-white coats, black eye masks and sweet natures. They were clever too. Charlie had taught them to do tricks. She said they could even count up to five. If only Summer could be so perfect and obedient.

'I had to escape our madhouse,' explained Charlie. 'Can you imagine five kids and all our animals cooped up inside? Zorro and Bandit were desperate for a good run.'

'It's no better at our place,' I said. 'All of us plus Summer the Wicked in our teensy caravan. It's been crazy.'

'What has the terror been up to now?' asked Charlie with a chuckle.

'You don't want to know!' I assured her.

But Charlie did, so I told her the long, sorry tale of Cici's demolished sandal and Bella's extinct dinosaurs. Charlie laughed and laughed.

It felt good to share the story with someone who understood.

'Summer might have done everyone a favour by eating Bella's dinosaurs,' joked Charlie.

'True! It'll be a lot quieter without so much roaring and stomping,' I agreed.

'Well, I'm glad Cici's not mad at you but it's pretty tough to have all your savings wiped out.'

I shrugged. 'I can always earn more by helping Mum at the Beach Shack. But let's hope Summer doesn't destroy anything else.'

Charlie tickled Bandit under the chin.

'She will,' Charlie assured me. 'You wouldn't believe how naughty Zorro and Bandit were when they were little.'

'Really?' I asked. The two dogs looked up at me as if to say, 'Us? Never!'

'Bandit used to steal everything – shoes, phone chargers, socks, dirty undies – even books,' said Charlie. 'That's how she got her name. Zorro was pretty wild too. Once I left Archie's saddle on the ground and they ripped it to shreds. It was months before they calmed down.'

'Terrific!' I said, imagining months to come of Summer destroying shoes, toys and toilet rolls. It would cost a fortune.

We'd arrived at the gate of Mimi and Papa's little white cottage. The house was half hidden by the lush garden of palm trees, frangipanis and hibiscus. A wisteria vine grew all over the front veranda, with clusters of purple flowers dangling like chandeliers. Our caravan was parked around the back.

'Would you like to come in?' I asked Charlie. Up until now I'd avoided asking the girls back here. We usually hung out at the cafe. In the beginning I had been embarrassed that we lived in a tiny, crowded caravan in the back garden of my grandparents' house. Now I knew the girls well enough to realise that it didn't matter anymore.

'Sure,' said Charlie. 'I'll put the dogs on the veranda, away from Summer, since she's not old enough to make friends yet.'

We tied Bandit and Zorro to a post under cover and went around the back. The rain had finally stopped, but the sky was still misty and grey.

First we went to the caravan so I could show Charlie where we were living. Mum was back from the shops and was unpacking the groceries, tucking things away in the tiny cupboards above the kitchen sink.

'Hello, Charlie,' said Mum. 'How lovely to see you.'

We chatted to Mum for a few moments. Charlie gazed around with interest, taking note of the bunks where Harry and I slept, and the double bed that Mum and Bella shared.

'Charlie's come to help me train Summer,' I explained. I took a deep breath. I hoped Mum wouldn't be cross about Summer's shoe-eating spree. 'Speaking of Summer, she did get into a little trouble today.'

Mum raised her eyebrow and closed the cupboard door. 'What wickedness has that puppy been up to now?'

I explained all about the jewelled sandal and going around to Cici's house to confess and giving up my pocket money to pay for new ones.

'That was exactly the right way to fix it, Pippa,' said Mum, looking at me with approval. 'I'm really proud of you.'

Mum might not be so proud of me in a minute, I thought to myself. I hesitated again.

'That's not all,' I said. Charlie gave me an encouraging smile. 'Summer also ate one of your shoes the other day and I hid them. I didn't want you to be cross with her.'

I dug Mum's favourite pair of shoes out of the back of the clothes cupboard. One shoe was perfect and the other utterly ruined.

Mum shook her head ruefully as she examined the tiny tooth marks. 'I was wondering where these were. It's just as well that Charlie's come over to help with Summer's schooling. The sooner we can break her shoe-chewing habit the better!'

Charlie and I laughed. I was so relieved that Mum wasn't cross or upset.

'Why don't we get started,' suggested Charlie. 'Looks like we have a *lot* of work to do!'

Charlie and I went inside Mimi and Papa's cottage. Harry and Bella were still trying to watch the movie but Summer was making it almost impossible, tumbling and whirling like a demented ballerina.

'Can you take her away, *pleeeaase*?' begged Bella. 'We can't concentrate on the movie.'

I scooped Summer up in my arms and we

took her out to the garden. I grabbed a pock-etful of doggy kibble on the way so we could reward her. Summer jumped down onto the paved patio. She raced around sniffing and wagging her tail then ran straight towards me.

Summer bowed forward, stretching her front legs and sticking her backside up in the air.

'She's bowing to me,' I said to Charlie, as I curtseyed back.

'That's puppy language for "let's play",' said Charlie.

'Summer? Do you want to play football?' I called, picking up a ball that was lying on the lawn. Summer looked up at me with her head cocked to one side and made a whimpering, talking sound.

'That's puppy language for "what's up?"' said Charlie.

'Let's go,' I said. Summer bounded forward with her ears pricked as if to say, 'At last! Time to have some fun.'

We started playing. It was the most hilarious football game because our teammate was a chubby puppy who didn't know any of the rules. I kicked the ball and Summer chased after it, her tail wagging madly. She bit the ball, which was bigger than she was. She growled and shook it from side to side.

Charlie grabbed the ball from Summer and kicked it back to me. We sent it scooting back and forth between us as Summer dashed this way and that, yipping with delight.

When Summer had burned up some energy, we practised her puppy training. She would come, sit, stay, and drop down, then eagerly gobble up her kibble as a reward. Finally, Charlie showed me how to teach her to walk on a lead. Summer trotted along beside Charlie like an angel. We made a big fuss of her.

Summer rolled on her back with all four paws in the air and whined.

'That's puppy for "please rub my tummy",'

said Charlie, bending down to do just that. I joined in.

'You really can speak puppy language!' I said. 'You can help me draw a puppy dictionary so I can understand what Summer's trying to tell me.'

Charlie laughed. 'You'd be surprised how fast Summer learns to understand English. Zorro and Bandit know so much. Mum says that border collies can learn over two hundred words.'

In the kitchen we sat at the table and chatted. I pulled my notebook out of my backpack and began to draw my puppy dictionary.

Charlie and I discussed different puppy poses and what they meant while I tried to capture them in doodle form.

'It's amazing,' I said. 'You're like Doctor Dolittle – you can talk with the animals.'

Charlie beamed with pleasure. She picked Summer up and cuddled her.

'When I grow up, I'd love to be a vet,' confided Charlie. 'I like helping sick and injured animals.'

'You'd make a good vet,' I agreed.

'But Mum says you need to be really good at maths and science to be a vet,' said Charlie. 'I like science but I'm totally hopeless at maths.'

I'd marked some of Charlie's maths papers and it definitely wasn't her best subject.

'You're not hopeless,' I said. 'You just need to work at it. Maths is pretty easy once you get the hang of it.'

'*Pfft,*' Charlie huffed.

'It's just practice,' I said. 'It's like me learning to surf. You've been doing it for so long that it comes naturally, but I'm hopeless. But the only way to get better is to keep working at it.'

Charlie chewed her lip. 'Maybe you're right.'

'Of course I'm right.' I whacked Charlie gently on the shoulder. 'I can help you with your maths if you like?'

Charlie leaned forward, her face alive with enthusiasm. 'That would be great. I look at the numbers and they make no sense to me at all!'

'I'd love to help,' I replied. 'We'll make a maths whizz out of you in no time.'

Charlie put Summer back down on the floor.

'What about you?' Charlie asked. 'Is there something you'd like to do when you grow up?'

'Sometimes I think I'd like to be an engineer,' I said. 'I love maths and figuring out how stuff works. I think it would amazing to design things and then build them.'

'That sounds really cool,' said Charlie. 'Maybe in the future you'll invent fantastic devices to help the world. Like personal jetpacks, or robots to clean up pollution, or self-sufficient buildings . . .'

I laughed. 'I think a robot who could do my homework would be perfect!'

CHAPTER 16

MONDAY MISERY

By lunchtime on Monday, the sky had finally cleared. The ground dried out like magic in the hot tropical sun. The four of us ate our lunches in our usual spot, under the shade of the large, spreading fig tree. The air was sticky and humid after the rain and we all felt sluggish and slow.

After a good night's sleep, yesterday's disaster didn't feel so grim anymore. Cici even made a joke about Summer being more passionate about shoes than her.

I checked my watch. 'It's time for our news-paper meeting in the library.'

I stood up. Meg, Cici and Charlie glanced at each other. Meg wrinkled her nose. I could tell that they weren't very keen.

'It's too hot,' complained Meg grumpily.

'There's not much point going,' said Cici. 'We didn't get many photos, so there's not enough to work on. We might as well just stay here and relax.'

For a moment I felt tempted to sit back and stretch out in the shade. But then I thought of how much work we still had to do and how many things had gone wrong already.

'We should go to the meeting,' I said firmly. 'The others will be wondering where we are and there might be something we can do to help. Besides, the weather's cleared so if we're organised we can take the photos after school.'

'Charlie and I have music lessons straight after school,' said Cici.

'Yes, but you finish by four o'clock. We could do it after that,' I reminded them. 'The light will be better later.'

The girls stayed sitting cross-legged for a moment.

'Okay,' said Charlie, slowly getting to her feet. 'I guess you're right.'

As we stood up, Olivia arrived with Sienna, Willow and Tash.

'Aren't you coming to the newspaper meeting?' asked Meg. 'It's due to start any minute.'

Olivia tossed her ponytail and glanced away. 'No, we've decided not to go.'

I remembered that the girls must be hugely disappointed that Ruby Starr hadn't come along to do the interview on Friday.

'You should come,' I said sympathetically.

Willow shook her head. 'Our story didn't work so we're dropping out of the club.'

'But you could do another story,' I said. 'There are still pages to fill.'

Oliva glared at me furiously. 'Why don't *you* do the extra pages?' she asked. 'It's all because your stupid cafe was too crowded that Ruby decided not to come.'

'What do you mean?' I asked.

'Ruby's agent told Dad that she walked right inside the Beach Shack,' said Olivia. 'Then she left because it was packed with people expecting to see her.'

I looked at Olivia in horror. 'But . . . you can't blame me! It wasn't my fault that half of Kira Cove School turned up to see her. It wasn't me who told them.'

'You couldn't bear us having a better idea than you,' snapped Olivia. 'You just had to spoil it.'

'I . . . I didn't do anything,' I stuttered.

Willow looked embarrassed by Olivia's outburst. 'We know it's not your fault,' she said, trying to restore the peace. 'We just don't feel like being in the newspaper club now.'

My friends and I walked to the library in silence. I was feeling upset by Olivia's accusation, even though Willow had apologised for her. And I was hugely disappointed that our plans to have fun working on the paper had backfired. Everything seemed to be going wrong.

Meg slipped her arm through mine. She always seemed to know when someone was feeling miserable. 'Don't worry about Olivia. She didn't really mean it.'

'I don't know why she still hates me so much,' I moaned. 'I can't do anything right around Olivia.'

'She doesn't hate you,' said Charlie, giving me a hug. 'She just wanted to be the star of the club by scooping the front-page story. Now she's mad at everyone – but mostly herself, I bet.'

'Charlie's right,' said Cici. 'Don't let Olivia bother you.'

My friends' concern did make me feel better. I gave them a small smile. 'Thanks.'

Inside the library, Jack and Seb were with a group of year six students working on a storyboard for the newspaper. A few of the other kids were also noticeably absent.

Jack and Seb looked very glum.

'Glad you four haven't dropped out as well,' said Jack. 'Looks like we've lost half our cub reporters.'

Mrs Neill looked up from her desk. 'I hope we'll have enough stories for our first issue.'

Seb shook his head. 'Not at this rate. Right now we have a super-skinny newspaper.'

'There are a few sport stories for the back pages but our front-page story fell through, and we don't have quite as much variety as we'd hoped,' said Lucy, one of the other year six editors.

Mrs Neill frowned. 'I promised Mrs Black

we'd have the first issue printed and ready to hand out on Thursday.'

We crowded around and looked at the story-board. There wasn't much besides a few stories about surfing, sailing and sport. But even that was slim, as the Saturday touch football games had been cancelled due to the rain.

'How did you guys go with your photo shoot on the weekend?' asked Seb. 'Do you have the story ready?'

We all shook our heads. 'The rain was a problem for us too. We only got a few photos,' explained Cici. 'Nowhere near enough for our story.'

All the year six students looked disappointed.

'But we're going to finish it this afternoon,' I assured them. 'We'll have something fantastic by Thursday.'

'That's good news,' said Seb. 'But we still need some more articles.'

Meg had the memory stick with the photos

we'd taken on the weekend, plus a bundle of our scribbled notes. The four of us sat around a computer and uploaded all our photos.

Once we'd deleted all my headless, blurry shots, we had three or four good ones. Meg dancing in the rain. Alex kicking the ball. Rory being chased up the beach by Charlie. The four of them soaked to the skin and laughing.

'It's a start,' I said optimistically.

'A teensy-weensy start,' agreed Cici. 'But nowhere near enough for two pages, let alone anything extra.'

Charlie thought for a moment, looking at the photos. She called over to Alex and Rory, who were working at the table next to us.

'Boys, what's your favourite food?' she asked, her green eyes alight with mischief.

'Pizza,' said Rory.

'Mum's roast lamb with crispy potatoes,' answered Alex.

'And ice-cream flavour?' asked Charlie.

'Vanilla,' said Alex.

'Nah – strawberry's the best,' replied Rory.

Charlie scribbled down the answers.

'So what do you want to do when you grow up?' asked Charlie.

'Be a video game designer,' said Rory. 'Or a computer programmer.'

'Ummm – maybe a professional football player or a chef,' said Alex. 'Why?'

Charlie turned to us triumphantly.

'Mrs Neill said she wanted us not to do an ordinary fashion shoot but to make the story more meaningful. So why don't we combine the photo shoot of kids wearing their favourite clothes, doing something they love, with a series of interviews about what they are passionate about? Like food, ice-cream, hobbies and the future?'

I turned to Charlie and smacked her on the arm. 'What an absolutely brilliant idea. Let's do it!'

Charlie threw her plait over her shoulder, grabbed a piece of paper and started writing. Then she snatched another blank sheet and wrote out the same thing all over again.

This is what Charlie wrote:

WHAT KIDS LOVE QUESTIONNAIRE

Name:

Age:

Favourite food?

Favourite ice-cream flavour?

Favourite hobbies?

What do you want to be when you grow up?

Favourite pets?

Favourite saying?

'What *are* you doing, Charlie?' asked Cici.

'She's writing a questionnaire for kids to fill in for our story,' I said.

'Exactly,' said Charlie. 'Now if we all fill in a questionnaire, then each ask two kids to do one too – we'll have twelve interviews in no time at all. We'd just need to type them up.'

'Genius,' said Meg. 'That would give us heaps.'

I helped Charlie photocopy multiple copies of her questionnaire and hand them out.

We all took one and began to fill it in. Meg chewed on her pen as she thought about her favourite saying. This is what she wrote:

Name: Meg

Age: 11

Favourite food? Roast chicken with baked potatoes and salad

Favourite ice-cream flavour? Vanilla-and-raspberry swirl

Favourite hobbies? Anything in the water – surfing, swimming, sailing and kayaking

What do you want to be when you grow up? A wildlife photographer and volunteer ranger working with African elephants, rhinoceros, mountain gorillas, leatherback turtles or Sumatran tigers

Favourite pets? Our ship's cat called Neptune, who sleeps on my bunk in the crook of my knees, and a pod of wild dolphins who visit us off the back of our yacht. My special dolphins are a mother and son called Artemis and Jupiter.

Favourite saying: Girls will save the world!

Meg finished hers and started jotting some notes on a piece of paper. I peered over her shoulder.

'Are you writing something else?' I asked.

'When Jack and Seb said they needed more stories for the newspaper it reminded me about my original idea,' said Meg. 'I may not be the best writer, but I'm definitely going to write a piece about endangered rhinos. Kids need to know.'

I gave Meg a hug. 'Absolutely! You'll do it perfectly. And if you need any help just ask me.'

CHAPTER 17

BEST FRIENDS EVER

By the end of the school day we had a pile of What Kids Love interviews typed up on the computer and ready for the newspaper.

The Wildlife Warrior had been busy too. Meg had been to visit the office staff and installed a fundraising box by the front door next to a giant poster. She'd also written a short story during class time and found some photos on the internet. Meg had asked me to help her edit the story. I'd suggested a couple of ideas for the phrasing but she'd already done a really good job.

SAVE THE RHINO BEFORE IT'S TOO LATE

By Megan O'Loughlin

One of the coolest animals on the planet is the rhinoceros. Rhinoceros (which means nose-horn) are plant-eating mammals with one or two horns on their noses. They live in the grasslands and forests of Africa and Asia and are closely related to horses.

Rhinos can weigh over 3500 kilograms and are the second largest land animal after the elephant. Sadly, rhinos are in danger of becoming extinct.

More rhinos are killed each year than are born. One rhino is killed every six hours every single day. There are only 5000 black rhinos left in the wild. Even worse, there are only 100 Sumatran rhinos and only 58 Javan rhinos left (making them the rarest land mammal on earth).

Rhinos are killed for their horns, which are used in traditional Chinese medicine. Rhino horn is worth more money per kilo than gold. Yet rhino horn is made of a protein called keratin, which is exactly the same as fingernails and hair. The horn is wrongly believed to be able to treat headaches and fever. That's as crazy as thinking that chewing your nails will fix your cold.

If poaching continues, rhinos will be extinct before you finish high school. This would be terrible!

What can we do? We can raise money to protect rhinos from poachers and to educate the public about the importance of saving endangered animals. Donate your pocket money or do some odd jobs to raise extra cash. There's a collection box in the office for the Kira Cove School Save-the-Rhino Fund.

Join the fight! Kids can change the world.

'This is a fantastic story, Meg,' I said. 'I'm going to donate the next money I earn from working at the cafe.'

'I have some pocket money from helping Mum with chores at home,' said Charlie.

'Me too,' said Cici. 'You were right, Meg. It's important for kids to know what's going on in the world.'

Meg beamed with pleasure. 'Thanks, Cici. Thanks, girls.'

Jack and Seb were so happy when we told them about our extra stories and photographs. The year six kids had come up with some more articles too. It looked like we might have enough for the newspaper to be printed on Thursday.

Now we needed to do our photo shoot so we met at the Beach Shack with all our stuff after Charlie and Cici's music lessons.

This time the sky was a deep clear blue and the sun shone down in true Kira style. Small waves lapped at the coral-white sand and gulls wheeled above. The late afternoon light was rich and golden.

Meg and Charlie rode their bikes – Meg carrying her surfboard under one arm and Charlie her precious guitar on her back. Cici's mum dropped her off with all the bags, Muffin and some props.

'Don't worry,' said Cici, unloading the back of her mum's stylish 4WD wagon. 'I've brought some sustenance along too. I invented an amazing new cupcake recipe yesterday when it was raining. I think you're going to love them!'

Cici had chosen the outfits for each shot and styled them with jewellery or fun accessories. There were white and denim shorts with floral tops and coloured singlets, skirts with bold prints, gypsy tops and ruffled skirts, and loads of floaty summer dresses that fluttered in the ocean breeze.

We got to work setting up shots.

Meg took photos of Cici and Charlie riding their skateboards down the esplanade with Muffin running along on her lead. We danced to our favourite song on the grass, singing into our water bottles. Charlie and I did handstands and cartwheels on the beach, sand sprinkling around our heads like fairy dust.

I took photos of Meg running towards the sea with her surfboard and riding her bike under the palm trees. I snapped close-ups of Muffin playing tug-of-war with Cici, Charlie's anklet and Cici's charm bracelet.

As Charlie, Meg and I skipped in the shallows, Meg grabbed my hand and pointed. A grey head appeared in the wave. Then another and another. It was Kira's pod of dolphins riding the waves. They skimmed and surfed, grinning at us.

'There's Artemis, and baby Jupiter,' said Meg. Meg could tell her favourite dolphins apart by the scars and notches on their fins.

We stood in the water silently and watched the beautiful scene. The Kira dolphins always filled me with delight.

As the sun started to sink in the west, Charlie sat on the rocks playing her guitar. She wore a white lace top, a ruffled amethyst skirt and had bare feet. With her long, golden hair she looked like a mermaid, just like Cici always said. Charlie began to sing one of her favourite Ruby Starr songs, 'Best Friends Ever', the melody floating out over the cove.

An older girl was walking by on the espla-nade, wearing big dark sunglasses and a floppy black hat. She stopped to listen to the song for a few minutes. When Charlie finished singing, Cici, Meg and I clapped.

'I love that song,' I said. 'You sang it beautifully, Charlie.'

The girl came down onto the beach, her cowboy boots sinking into the soft sand.

'That was fantastic,' she said. I suddenly recognised her as the girl who'd come just inside the cafe on Friday afternoon. She was wearing a different top, but the same ripped jeans and sunglasses.

'You have a lovely voice,' said the girl. 'And I like the song you chose.'

'Thanks,' said Charlie, tucking the pick under the strings of her guitar. Charlie looked closely at the girl. She suddenly went pale then bright pink. 'Oh my goodness – you're . . . you're Ruby Starr.'

Ruby smiled shyly, taking off her sunglasses. 'Yes. And I can't tell you what a thrill it was to hear you playing one of my songs.'

'You're my favourite singer,' said Charlie. 'We all love your songs.'

We each introduced ourselves to Ruby Starr and chatted with her about ourselves, our dogs, and what she was doing back in Kira Cove.

'I'm visiting for my mum's birthday,' said Ruby, giving Muffin a scratch behind the ears, 'but I can only stay a few more days. Would you like me to sing something for you?'

'Yes, *please*,' we all shrieked together.

Ruby sat on the rock next to Charlie and borrowed her guitar.

'Would you mind if I took some photos, please, Ruby?' asked Meg. 'We're doing a photo shoot for our school newspaper on "What Kids Love" – and I can tell you that pretty much all of the kids at school adore you.'

Ruby glowed. 'Of course you can. I'd love to be part of your story.'

After strumming a few chords, Ruby began

to sing the song that we had danced to at school with Miss Demi. It was an upbeat song called 'Love and Laughter'.

I wanted to pinch myself to make sure I wasn't dreaming it all. I couldn't believe that I was sitting on the sand, listening to Ruby Starr herself, singing a song that we all loved. Meg, Cici and I grinned at each other, our heads bobbing and our feet jiggling. Charlie sat on the rock next to Ruby, completely mesmerised. Meg took some more photos.

'How about a fun selfie?' suggested Cici. So we all crowded around and pulled silly faces while Meg snapped the picture.

'We're about to go and have some afternoon tea,' said Charlie, hopefully. 'Would you like to join us?'

Ruby looked like she was going to say no.

'We're going to my mum's cafe, just here,' I said, pointing at the Beach Shack. 'It's closed because it's after five o'clock, but Mum said we could use it as a base for our photo shoot. She'll be there packing up.'

'We have homemade cupcakes,' said Cici enticingly. 'I heard a rumour that you like those!'

'I certainly do,' Ruby admitted. 'My mum and I had coffee and lemon cupcakes at your cafe last week to celebrate her birthday. I thought it was wonderful. I remember when that boatshed really was just a beach shack.'

So we all went inside and sat at the long kitchen bench. Mum and Zoe were just finishing up. I made us all chocolate milkshakes with extra syrup and Cici put out a platter of her latest invention – strawberry cream cupcakes.

Each little cake had a syrupy strawberry baked inside and was topped with fresh whipped cream and two slivers of strawberry, perched like a red butterfly on top.

'These are delicious,' said Ruby. 'They're even better than the lemon cupcakes I had here last week. And that's saying something!'

'Mmmmm,' I agreed, my mouth full of scrumptiousness.

'Smile,' said Meg, snapping more photos of us scoffing strawberry delights.

Charlie gazed at Ruby adoringly. 'I just can't believe I'm sitting here, eating afternoon tea with my favourite singer. And we have photographs to remember it by.'

Cici grinned. 'This story will definitely be big enough for the front page!'

I felt a flicker of glee at the thought. Then I realised that we were actually stealing Olivia, Sienna, Willow and Tash's story idea, which made me feel a little guilty at the same time.

'Olivia will be furious!' I said.

'Definitely,' said Cici, with a wicked glint in her eye.

'And what about the kids who hoped to meet Ruby at the cafe last Friday?' said Meg, with far more sympathy. 'They were all so disappointed.'

'Who was hoping to meet me?' asked Ruby.

I quickly explained about the word getting out about the interview and how they all turned up to catch a glimpse of their favourite pop star. 'The kids at Kira Cove were desperate to see you.'

Ruby looked thoughtful. 'I didn't think about it like that. I told my agent I'd do the interview with the girls as a favour but no one was supposed to know I'd be at the cafe. I've been trying to lie low, see my family and rest before my tour starts. When I saw the big crowd at the cafe I panicked and imagined there might be paparazzi or journalists from the mainland there.'

Ruby looked around at each of us and pulled a wry face. 'A couple of weeks ago, I had photographers camping in the front garden of my apartment block. Some crazy rumour was flying around and so they were stalking me everywhere. I had to climb down the fire escape to go out.'

'It must be hard being famous sometimes,' I said.

'Don't get me wrong,' said Ruby. 'I love performing and meeting my fans. I hate to think that all those kids came to see me and were disappointed because I didn't turn up.'

'At least they'll be able to read about you in the school newsletter,' said Charlie. 'Do you mind, Ruby, if we asked you a couple of questions for our story?'

Ruby put down her cupcake, looking wary. I remembered Olivia's plan to ask her about breaking up with her boyfriend, Kai Stone. Ruby must get asked very personal questions all the time. No wonder she looked so apprehensive.

'What sort of questions?' replied Ruby.

'Like what's your favourite ice-cream flavour?' asked Charlie.

CHAPTER 18

RIPTIDE

On Tuesday afternoon, I went to meet Meg and Jack at the beach. Meg had promised to give me another surfing lesson. I was still buzzing with the excitement of yesterday afternoon. I'm pretty sure that it was one of the best days of my life. Well, not counting the day we started the Sassy Sisters – and the day Mum gave us a new puppy!

I packed Mum's camera in my backpack, hoping to practise taking some more action photos.

Meg and Jack were once again waiting for me on the wall near the surf lifesaving club. They were dressed in their wetsuits, with their boards all ready to go. Mariana was sitting on a park bench nearby, reading a book.

I didn't have a wetsuit so I wore my horrid old navy-blue swimming costume under my beach dress. It looked like I'd be wearing this costume for a long time to come – thanks to mischievous Miss Summer!

'Sorry, Pippa,' Meg said. 'But I've got some bad news – the surf's picked up this afternoon. I think it's too big for you to go out today.'

I felt disappointed as I'd really been looking forward to my next lesson with Meg and Jack. But I knew Meg wouldn't go back on our plans unless she had a good reason to.

'Don't worry, we can do it another day,' I replied.

'We can go for a walk or something instead,' said Meg. But I could tell by the way she was looking out at the waves that she was keen to surf.

'No, you don't need to stay with me,' I said. 'Go with Jack. I'll take some photos of you guys.'

Jack grinned at me. 'Make sure you catch my good side!'

'You don't have a good side,' teased Meg, whacking him on the shoulder.

Meg did up her leg-rope and looked out to sea. She frowned.

'Pippa, don't go swimming here,' warned Meg. 'There's a nasty rip running out just there.'

'Are you sure?' I said, scanning the crashing waves. 'It doesn't look dangerous.'

Jack pointed directly in front of us. 'Remember what Meg said the other day? Look for where the water is flatter.'

'Oh, yes. I see it now.'

Jack ran off towards the water, his leg-rope looping down from his board.

'Will you be okay?' asked Meg. 'I can stay here with you on the beach if you like?'

'No, thanks, Meg,' I replied. 'I'll be fine.'

'We won't be long,' said Meg. 'The waves are just too good to resist.'

I sat on my towel watching Jack and Meg paddle out through the waves. They sat on their boards bobbing up and down out the back, behind the breaking waves. I took out Mum's camera and started snapping some shots, first of Meg and then of Jack surfing towards the shore.

A family arrived and set up a few metres down the beach from me. There was a mother with three children, two girls and a boy. The kids looked to be between five and eight years old. They stretched out their towels, slathered on sunscreen and began building a sandcastle together.

Meg caught a long wave and skimmed along the glassy wall of water. I clicked away, using the lens to get as close as I could. Meg was graceful and lithe as she zoomed along, her dark hair sleek as a porpoise.

Out of the corner of my eye I saw the three children run down to the sea to paddle, their mother following more slowly behind. They jumped into the water, right near the sandy current that Jack and Meg had warned me about. The kids shrieked with excitement as the cold waves splashed over them.

I stood up, not sure what to do. Surely the mother would notice and stop them before they got too far out? But it looked like she hadn't seen the rip.

'Not too far out,' called the mother. 'Wait for me.'

The waves sucked out, leaving the sand sparkling in the sunshine. The three children ran further towards the retreating sea.

'Careful,' I called out to them. 'There's a rip just –'

But before I could finish my sentence, a large wave roared towards the shore. It knocked the two older children sprawling, dragging them underwater. Their mother raced out to rescue them. She grabbed hold of her youngest daughter. Another wave followed, smashing into them too and sweeping the whole family out of the shallows and into the rip.

I stood frozen for a moment, not knowing what to do.

The four heads bobbed up above the surface. They began to swim towards the shore, but the current was too strong. They were being dragged further and further out. The mother raised her arm in the air and waved. 'Help. Help us!'

If I went in after the family, I would be sucked out to sea too. Should I run for help?

I stared all around for someone, anyone who could help. Mariana was too far away, sitting on the esplanade, reading her book. The only people within shouting distance were Jack and Meg. I waved my arms back and forth, shouting to get their attention.

'Meg! Jack! There's a family caught in the rip!' I pointed to where the family were struggling and thrashing in the water. One of the smaller heads disappeared under the water. The mother dived under and dragged her child to the surface, but she couldn't possibly hold all three children up at once.

Thank goodness Jack and Meg heard me. The two of them began paddling furiously towards the distressed family. By now the four heads were about a hundred metres offshore. Then I remembered that the surf lifesaving club was not far up the beach. There would be someone there who could help us.

I dropped mum's camera onto my backpack and raced up the beach as fast as I could.

There were three lifesavers sitting under the shelter, watching the swimmers between the flags. One was Zoe and another was her patrol captain, Nigel.

'Zoe, help,' I yelled. 'There's a family in trouble down the beach.'

Zoe and Nigel leapt into action, grabbing lifebelts, radios and paddleboards. I leaned over with my hands on my knees, trying to catch my breath. But I only rested for a moment. I was too worried about the young family. I turned and raced back all the way down the beach to where I'd left them.

The three lifesavers jogged more slowly, lugging two rescue boards and all their gear.

By the time I returned, Meg and Jack had reached the family out the back behind the waves. The four swimmers were clinging to the sides of the surfboards. Jack had the mother and the youngest child, while Meg had the boy and the older girl. Jack hauled the little one out of the sea and onto the surfboard in front of him. Meg and Jack began slowly paddling for the shore with all their might, hampered by the extra weight.

The lifesavers reached me and stripped off to their swimming costumes. Zoe's face, normally happy and smiley, looked tense and focused.

'Don't try to paddle ashore,' yelled Nigel to Jack and Meg. 'Stay where you are and keep calm. We're coming to get you.'

He turned to the others. 'Zoe, come with me. Lisa, you stay here with the radio and stand by in case we need to call an ambulance.'

Zoe and Nigel pushed the rescue boards into the sea, jumped on and paddled with all their might.

My heart was thumping with anxiety as I waited on the shore. I felt so useless. Would Zoe and Nigel get to them in time? Would Meg and Jack be able to keep the family afloat? I needed something to distract me.

I looked around and saw Mum's camera sitting where I'd left it on top of my backpack.

I picked it up and started snapping photographs of the action.

Zoe and Nigel powered through the water, racing to reach the bobbing surfboards with their precious cargo. Through the zoom lens, I could see Meg's face, pale and tense as she struggled to keep the surfboard steady. The older girl lost her grip and Meg had to drag her back towards the board. Jack had his own struggle with the youngest child, who wriggled and cried with terror, nearly slipping into the sea.

It took long, tense minutes for Zoe and Nigel to reach the group. Nigel took command, calling instructions and transferring the children to his rescue board. Zoe scooped up the youngest child and hauled her onto her own board.

Together the lifesavers, Meg and Jack brought the family into the beach. A wave gathered momentum and surged towards the sand, carrying the boards with it. Nigel waded ashore with a child under each arm.

Zoe carried the youngest child in her arms. The little girl was pale and shaking, coughing up seawater. Jack and Meg helped the mother, who was visibly exhausted and collapsed on the sand. After a couple of minutes she sat up and wept as she hugged her children close.

Zoe and Lisa set to work checking the children for injuries and shock. Thankfully they were all okay. Jack and Meg had reached them in time to prevent any serious damage. We helped Nigel to drag all the boards onto the sand then stood around watching as the life-savers worked calmly and efficiently.

'Are you feeling all right?' Zoe asked the mother.

'It all happened so fast,' she sobbed. 'I told the children they could go in up to their knees but the water rushed in so quickly. There was nothing I could do.'

'You're all okay,' said Nigel soothingly. 'Thanks to these two courageous surfers. And this young lady who ran for help.'

Zoe gave us all a hug. 'It may have ended very differently if you three hadn't been so quick thinking and brave.'

I felt shy and proud all at once. Jack, Meg and I grinned at each other.

Nigel and Zoe introduced all of us to the family.

'I'm Annetta Moretti,' said the mother. 'And this is Lucia, Marco and Aurora.'

Annetta turned to us. 'I can never thank you three enough. You saved our lives.'

'It was our pleasure,' said Jack. 'We were lucky to be out there when Pippa saw you get into trouble.'

'Well, Annetta, I do hope that you'll remember to swim between the flags in future,' said Nigel sternly. 'The ocean is very unpredictable.'

Annetta shuddered. 'Definitely. I won't ever

make that mistake again. I hate to think what might have happened.'

Nigel noticed the camera I was holding. 'Did you take some photographs of the rescue?'

'Yes,' I replied.

'Could you let me have some copies?' asked Nigel. 'I'd love to publish them in our club newsletter, if you don't mind?'

'Of course,' I replied. 'I don't know if they'll be any good. But I can email them to you.'

'Why don't I take a photograph of the three of you?' Zoe suggested.

So Meg, Jack and I posed with the two surf-boards and the ocean behind us. We had our arms around each other's necks and broad smiles on our faces. Then I took a photo of the brave lifesaving team with their red-and-yellow caps.

Annetta didn't want her children photo-graphed. They were still too shaken. However, she did give Nigel a lovely quote about us for the newsletter. Zoe recorded it on her phone. We all helped the family to pack up their beach gear and then Lisa and Nigel walked them back to the lifesaving club for a final check-up.

'Don't forget to send us copies of the photos,' said Zoe with a smile. 'You three were amazing!'

CHAPTER 19

SCOOP

After saying goodbye to my friends, I walked home thinking about what Nigel had said about including the photos in the club newsletter. Meg and Jack had been so incredibly brave to assist a whole family and keep them afloat for so long. They really were heroes.

Of course! I could write up a story on the rescue for the school newsletter to go with the photos. I raced home, got changed, then went to get Summer from Mimi's house.

Summer was super-excited to see me, rolling on her back and offering me her tummy to scratch.

I sat at the table in the caravan, with Summer at my feet, and set to work. I borrowed Mum's computer and loaded the photos from the camera onto the laptop. Summer nibbled my toes while I worked.

The photos came up clear and sharp, bringing the rescue back to life. I chose the four best photos, including the one of Meg, Jack and me with the surfboards on the shore, plus the group shot of the lifesavers.

I sat down and planned out the story, then I typed it up. I phoned Nigel at the surf club and asked him if I could get a few quotes. Then I rang Meg and Jack on their yacht.

I read over my story, then I rewrote and rewrote to make it as good as it could be. This is what I had written:

HEROIC RESCUE – KIRA KIDS SAVE FAMILY CAUGHT IN RIP

By Philippa Hamilton

Two Kira Cove primary school students have been praised as heroes after rescuing a family of swimmers caught in a rip. Sister and brother, Meg and Jack O'Loughlin, aged 11 and 12, were surfing off Kira Beach at around 4 pm on Monday afternoon, when a family in need of help was spotted from the shore.

A mother and her three young children were splashing in the shallows when a powerful wave swept them off the beach and out into deep water. The rip carried them a hundred metres offshore, where the mother tried to keep the children afloat.

Jack and Meg paddled about fifty metres to reach the struggling swimmers. They calmed the children and helped them to cling onto their surfboards until lifesavers Nigel Woods, Zoe Martin and Lisa Shehadie arrived to help bring the family back to shore.

'These kids deserve a medal for their bravery,' said Patrol Captain Nigel Woods. 'They stayed calm under pressure and put their own lives at risk to save the distressed swimmers. This incident is a timely reminder of the importance of always swimming between the patrol flags.'

The young surfers were humble about their involvement in the rescue.

'We are so glad that we were out surfing and there to help when it was needed,' said Meg O'Loughlin. 'It was a huge relief when the lifesavers arrived to help bring them to shore.'

Her brother Jack said he and his sister had to be careful to keep the swimmers still.

'It all happened so fast, we didn't have time to feel scared,' said Jack. 'We learn surf lifesaving skills at school so we knew we had to keep the kids calm so that they didn't panic and tip us off our boards.'

The mother of the young family, who has asked to remain anonymous, was very shaken but thankful.

'I hate to think what would have happened if Jack and Meg hadn't been there to save us,' she said. 'I will be eternally grateful to those brave young heroes.'

When I was sure that I was happy with it, I emailed the article to Jack and Seb. I sent it to Nigel too, along with the four best photographs. There, I'd done it. An extra story for the newspaper. And I had a hopeful feeling it was good – really good!

Mum arrived home with Bella and Harry a few minutes after I'd sent off the story, so I was bursting with news to tell them. Mum *oohed* and *aahed* as I recounted the dramatic rescue.

'Thank goodness you were there, Pipkin,' said Mum, blinking away tears. 'And Meg and Jack, and Zoe too. Otherwise goodness knows what might have happened to that poor family.'

Bella was jiggling up and down on the edge of the bed. Harry was lying on the floor playing with Summer's silky ears.

'That's not as exciting as what happened to me today,' said Bella. 'I met Ruby Starr! She came into the cafe. I told her all about how I'm going to be a palaeontologist or maybe an archaeologist.'

My heart sank. I imagined poor Ruby having her ear chewed off by my baby sister.

'Oh, yes, I completely forgot,' said Mum.

'Your friend Ruby came into the cafe this afternoon looking for you.'

'Looking for me?' I asked. 'I wonder why?'

Mum raised her eyebrows in a mysterious way. 'She's leaving to go on her world tour on Friday morning. But she came up with an idea she wanted to discuss with you and the girls.'

Mum paused, dragging out the suspense.

'And?' I demanded impatiently. 'What idea?'

'Ruby asked my permission first,' continued Mum. 'And I agreed. But perhaps it's best if you ring her and Ruby can tell you all about it herself.'

Mum passed me her mobile. 'She gave me her number but you mustn't tell anyone.'

By this time I was squirming with impatience. I grabbed the phone and hit the dial button.

'Hello,' answered the voice on the other end.

'Hi. Is that Ruby?' I asked. 'It's Pippa Hamilton here. Mum said you wanted to talk to me about something?'

'Thanks for calling, Pippa,' said Ruby. 'Yes. I had an idea and wanted to know what you think.'

Ruby explained her idea to me. It was a great idea. An absolutely fantastically incredible idea. The other Sassy Sisters would be ecstatic.

'We'd love to!' I said, barely containing my excitement. 'I'll ring the girls and we'll organise it straight away.'

CHAPTER 20

THE CONCH

After school on Thursday, the year six editors stood by the front gate with Mrs Neill, handing out copies of the very first issue of the Kira school newspaper.

'Here you go, girls,' said Mrs Neill, smiling at the four of us. 'Your very own copies of our *Kira Conch*. Thanks so much for your efforts. You all did a marvellous job with your stories.'

We each grabbed a copy of the newspaper.

My heart gave a skip of excitement when I saw the front cover.

'And I've decided to award you each a prize for the best story,' continued Mrs Neill. 'I know you all worked together very closely, so I have a special book pack for each of you in the library.'

'Thanks, Mrs Neill,' we chorused. But while it was fun to win the prize, holding the newspaper in my hand was the best reward for our hard work.

The newspaper's masthead was illustrated with a large, curly conch shell. Jack told me that in ancient times these shells were used as horns. On the top half of the front page was the photo Zoe had taken of Jack, Meg and myself at the beach with our arms around each other. Underneath it was the story that I had written. I noticed that Jack had made a few edits.

THE KIRA CONCH

KIRA COVE SCHOOL HEROES
SAVE FAMILY

By Philippa Hamilton

Three Kira Cove primary school students
have been praised for their heroic rescue
of a family who were swept out to sea in a
strong rip. Sister and brother, Meg and Jack
O'Loughlin, aged 11 and 12, were surfing
off Kira Beach around 4 pm on Monday
afternoon, when a family in need of help was
spotted from the shore by their friend, Kira
Conch reporter Pippa Hamilton.

Pippa was on the beach when she saw the
family being swept into the surf and called
for help. She then ran up the beach to fetch
the lifesavers . . .

I felt a huge thrill when I saw my name in print on the front page. The rest of the story was continued on page three, including the quote from Nigel praising all of us for our bravery and quick thinking. He called us young superheroes!

On the bottom half of the front page was a huge photo of Ruby Starr sitting on the rocks playing Charlie's guitar. The headline read:

RUBY STARR INSPIRES KIDS TO LOVE LIFE

Interview by Charlie Harper

There aren't many Kira Cove students who don't love the music of our very own pop star, Ruby Starr. So when our fave songstress popped home to the island for her mum's birthday, all the locals were dying to meet her. So far, Ruby's been lying low in preparation for her world tour, which kicks off in Sydney this Friday. But the good news is that before she jets off, Ruby will be hanging out at her favourite cafe – the Beach Shack – this evening. She has invited all the kids of Kira Cove School to come along to meet her at her farewell bash. Ruby will perform a couple of songs from her latest album and sign autographs from 4 pm to 5 pm. We look forward to seeing you there!

Before you meet Ruby, get to know her a little better with the questionnaire below.

Favourite food? Barbecued steak with mushroom sauce and mashed potatoes. Although Cici's strawberry cream cupcakes are pretty awesome too!

Favourite ice-cream flavour? Coffee

Favourite hobbies? Singing, dancing, playing the guitar and writing songs

What do you want to do in the future?
I want to make people happy through my music. I want my songwriting to make people think about the world and their place in it.

Favourite pets? I travel a lot so I really love coming home to our family dog, a bouncy Jack Russell called Pogo.

Favourite motto? *Live* every moment. *Laugh* every day. *Love* with all your heart. It was the inspiration behind my latest album.

There was eager muttering among the students as they read the news about Ruby performing at the Beach Shack this afternoon.

I was jittery with excitement.

You see, when I spoke to Ruby on the phone she had explained that she still felt terrible about all the kids who had left disappointed after coming to the Beach Shack to see her. She also felt really awful about Olivia, Tash, Willow and Sienna being so upset when she hadn't arrived for her interview.

So, as well as performing and signing autograhs at the Beach Shack, she would also have a special afternoon tea with Olivia, Sienna, Willow and Tash.

Charlie and I wandered over to where Olivia and her friends were talking to the boys in the playground. Some of the kids were holding copies of the newspaper and reading different stories.

'I can't believe it,' said Olivia, shaking the newspaper in disgust. 'I can't believe they stole our story idea.'

I looked at Charlie and raised my eyebrows in an 'I told you so' way.

'Olivia,' I said, as we joined the group. 'We didn't mean to steal your story.'

Olivia looked at Charlie and me as though we were slimy, green critters from Mars. She clearly didn't want us anywhere near her.

'It just kind of happened...' I tried to explain.

Olivia's face went bright red. 'As if you didn't plan it! You set out from the beginning to ruin it. You didn't want us to have the best story. You wanted to be the ones to get the front-page scoop.'

Everyone looked at me. I gulped.

'No, it wasn't like that, Olivia,' said Charlie.

'We honestly didn't plan to interview Ruby,' I said. 'We were just lucky that she walked by while Charlie was singing one of her songs.'

'Ruby was so excited,' Charlie added. 'Then we started chatting with her...'

'It was *my* father who found out that Ruby was coming home to Kira Island,' said Olivia, her eyes filling with tears. 'And it was *my* idea to interview her for the school newspaper. If she hadn't decided to do it at your cafe this would never have happened.'

I paused. Olivia was right. It was Olivia's

idea. She could never have guessed that so many people would turn up and that Ruby would panic and leave. It probably would have happened no matter where the interview was planned. I did feel sorry for Olivia and the girls.

'I know,' I said. 'It was a brilliant idea. And I'm sorry you were all so disappointed when Ruby didn't come into the Beach Shack that day.'

Olivia tossed her head and looked away, her arms crossed. She blinked back tears.

I pulled four envelopes out of my backpack.

'But I do have something for you from Ruby that might make up for it,' I said.

'What is it?' asked Tash, looking curiously at my fistful of envelopes.

'Open it,' I said, passing one each to Tash, Willow, Sienna and Olivia. The girls ripped them open and read the handwritten notes inside.

'What does it say?' asked Alex, peering over Tash's shoulder.

'Ruby Starr has personally written to ask the four of us to afternoon tea today at the Beach Shack,' explained Tash. 'She apologises for not making it last Friday and wants us to be the star guests at a special celebration.'

'And she wants to interview us,' said Olivia, with a high-pitched squeak of excitement. 'She wants to interview *us* for the next issue of *The Kira Conch*!'

'Ruby hates doing interviews herself,' explained Charlie. 'But we told her about how we'd come up with a set of questions about what kids love for the school newspaper. So she agreed to answer those questions for us, and thought she could ask you the same questions at afternoon tea.'

'So will you come?' I asked the girls.

'Of course we will!' they shrieked together.

CHAPTER 21

RUBY'S FAREWELL

A big group of us walked to the Beach Shack, joking and laughing. A stream of kids and their parents was already heading the same way.

A blackboard outside the cafe read:

> **Special performance today by Kira Cove's very own Ruby Starr. 4–5 pm. Everybody welcome!**

Inside, Mum and Zoe were super-prepared this time. Zoe's friend Lisa had come along to help in the kitchen.

The cafe was decorated with star-shaped bunting hanging from the ceiling and buckets of pink lilies, white orchids and crimson roses. A microphone and stool were set up in the middle of the cafe with two guitars leaning against the counter. A number of tables were already occupied with people eating, drinking and bubbling with anticipation.

Cici was there waiting for us, looking quite at home behind the counter. She was setting out an enormous platter of her new invention – Cici's strawberry cream cupcake delights. This batch had a berry-sweet, ruby-red star balanced on top of the whipped cream.

'They look perfect,' I said.

'Thanks,' said Cici, smiling. 'Zoe has reserved us some tables. I'll show you where to go.'

Olivia's gang sat at my favourite round table in the corner. We sat down at the table next to it. Crowds of kids and their parents wandered in and took seats where they could.

Zoe carried over a three-tiered cake stand full of strawberry cream cupcakes, blueberries and chicken-and-lettuce finger sandwiches for each table.

'This is so exciting,' said Zoe, as she returned with a tray of freshly blended pineapple juices. 'Ruby is upstairs getting ready.'

I noticed Mimi and Papa arrive with another couple, and Mum showed them to their table. 'That's Ruby's parents with your grandparents,' whispered Charlie. Mrs Beecham soon joined them.

Mum stopped by our table and gave us all a hug.

'Everything's ready,' said Mum. 'Looks like it's going to be a great afternoon.'

'All the kids are *sooo* excited to meet Ruby,' said Charlie.

'She should be coming down any second,' said Mum.

Sure enough, a ripple of excitement ran through the crowd as Ruby made her grand entrance. She was wearing a ruffled yellow dress sprigged with red flowers, cowboy boots and a garland of red roses in her hair. She waved to everyone then made her way to Olivia's table.

Ruby beamed at us and called hello before sitting down. Olivia, Sienna, Tash and Willow were almost jumping with happiness. Guests ate and drank and gossiped. The pile of strawberry cream cupcakes disappeared before our eyes.

The girls chatted with Ruby. I could hear them answering her interview questions for the next issue of *The Kira Conch*. The questions were the fun ones Charlie had come up with.

'My favourite food is beef tacos with guacamole and my favourite ice-cream is cookies-and-cream,' said Olivia.

'And Olivia, do you know what you might like to be when you're older?' asked Ruby.

Olivia thought for a moment. 'I would really love to be a doctor.'

'Fantastic, Olivia,' said Ruby. 'But why a doctor?'

'Doctors help people when they're sick or hurt,' said Olivia. 'They're kind and care about their patients. Like you said in your interview, Ruby – I'd really like to make the world a better place.'

'That is a truly wonderful dream, Olivia. I'm sure you'll make a fantastic doctor,' said Ruby, smiling at her. 'Now, I've loved chatting with you girls but it's time for me to take the microphone.'

Ruby walked up to the makeshift stage.

'Good afternoon to the lovely folk of Kira Island,' she said. There was a roar of approval from the crowd. 'Thank you all for making me feel so welcome back in my home town.'

Ruby's parents glowed with pride.

'Last week I was feeling sad,' Ruby explained. 'Things had not been so great. But a group of Kira Cove kids made me realise how very lucky I am. You reminded me what's important in my life – my family, friends, music and the Kira sunset.

'So I'd like you all to be the first to hear my latest song, "Kira Dreaming".'

Ruby picked up her guitar and began to sing a new song. Her voice was sweet and clear. We all listened closely. It was a song about treasuring friendship and chasing your dreams.

Then she sang 'Love and Laughter', the song we danced to at school. All the kids from school rose to their feet and many of them began to dance. When Ruby finished the song, I thought I saw tears running down her cheeks.

'Now I'd like to ask four girls to come up on stage with me,' she said. 'I hope that Charlie Harper will sing a song with me, with a little help from her best friends – Meg, Cici, and Pippa.'

Charlie blushed with pleasure. The four of us glanced at each other in shock. We were going to sing with Ruby Starr in front of everyone we knew. How exciting! How terrifying!

Ruby waved her arm to summon us. 'Come and join me, girls. Let's perform "Best Friends Ever", the perfect song for sharing on Kira Beach as the sun goes down.'

Ruby began strumming the opening chords.

Charlie grabbed my hand and we walked up to stand beside Ruby together, with Meg and Cici right behind us. Ruby began to sing and we all joined in. A song of love and joy and being best friends. It was the best song in the world.

CICI'S STRAWBERRY CREAM CUPCAKE RECIPE

Makes 12 regular cupcakes

¾ CUP OF CASTER SUGAR

2 CUPS OF SELF-RAISING FLOUR

125 GRAMS OF SOFTENED BUTTER

2 EGGS, LIGHTLY BEATEN WITH A FORK

¾ CUP OF MILK

1 TEASPOON OF VANILLA ESSENCE

1 PUNNET OF WHOLE STRAWBERRIES WITH TOPS SLICED OFF

STRAWBERRY CREAM

1 CUP OF HEAVY WHIPPING CREAM

3 TABLESPOONS OF SUGAR

VANILLA ESSENCE

6 TABLESPOONS OF PUREED STRAWBERRIES

1. PRE-HEAT OVEN TO 200 DEGREES CELSIUS.
2. LINE A MUFFIN PAN WITH PAPER PATTY CASES.
3. PLACE SUGAR AND FLOUR IN A BOWL AND MIX.
4. ADD BUTTER, EGGS, MILK, AND VANILLA ESSENCE AND COMBINE WELL.
5. SPOON MIXTURE INTO CUPCAKE PATTY CASES.
6. INSERT ONE WHOLE STRAWBERRY IN THE CENTRE OF EACH CUPCAKE AND RESERVE THE REST FOR TOPPING.
7. BAKE FOR 10–12 MINUTES UNTIL WELL-RISEN AND FIRM TO THE TOUCH.
8. ALLOW TO COOL IN THE PAN FOR FIVE MINUTES AND THEN TRANSFER TO A WIRE RACK TO COOL FULLY.
9. WHIP CREAM WITH SUGAR AND VANILLA ESSENCE THEN FOLD IN STRAWBERRY PUREE.
10. SPREAD EVENLY OVER EACH CUPCAKE.
11. TOP WITH A FRESH STRAWBERRY CUT IN HALF AND ARRANGED TO LOOK LIKE WINGS.

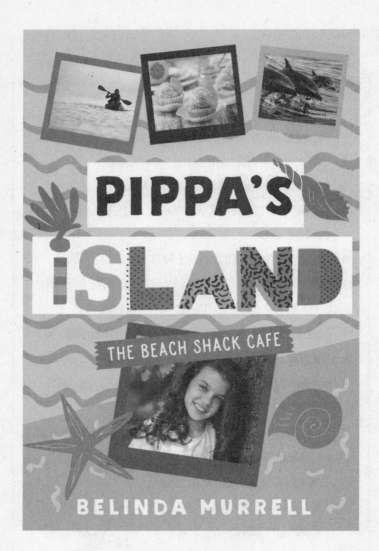

PIPPA'S iSLAND

THE BEACH SHACK CAFE

BELINDA MURRELL

THE BEACH SHACK CAFE

Pippa has just arrived at a new school, in a new town, and even living on a gorgeous island isn't cheering her up. Her arrival causes ripples at Kira Island Primary School – but Pippa soon starts to make friends with eco-warrior Meg, boho-chick Charlie, and fashionista and cupcake baker Cici.

Pippa's mum plans to buy a rustic old boatshed and start a bookshop cafe, and Pippa worries they'll lose all their money in this madcap venture – until her new friends come to the rescue to help get the grand opening back on track.

Will Kira Island ever feel like home?

OUT NOW

ABOUT THE AUTHOR

At about the age of eight, Belinda Murrell began writing stirring tales of adventure, mystery and magic in hand-illustrated exercise books. As an adult, she combined two of her great loves – writing and travelling the world – and worked as a travel journalist, technical writer and public relations consultant. Now, inspired by her own three children, Belinda is a bestselling, internationally published children's author. Her previous titles include four picture books, her fantasy adventure series, The Sun Sword Trilogy, and her seven time-slip adventures, *The Locket of Dreams, The Ruby Talisman, The Ivory Rose, The Forgotten Pearl, The River Charm, The Sequin Star* and *The Lost Sapphire*.

For younger readers (aged 6 to 9), Belinda has the Lulu Bell series about friends, family, animals and adventures growing up in a vet hospital.

Belinda lives in Manly in a gorgeous old house overlooking the sea with her husband, Rob, her three beautiful children, Sammy the Stimson's python and her dog, Rosie. She is an Author Ambassador for Room to Read and Books in Homes.

Find out more about Belinda at her website: **www.belindamurrell.com.au**

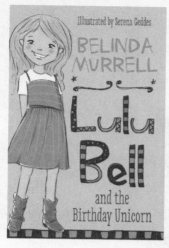

Adventures are more fun with friends!
There are thirteen gorgeous Lulu Bell
stories for you to discover.

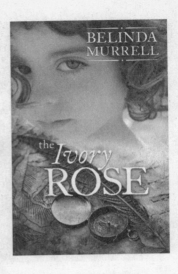

Love history? Escape to another time
with Belinda's seven beautiful
time-slip adventures.

If you love fantasy stories, you'll love
Belinda's Sun Sword trilogy.